ANDREO'S RACE

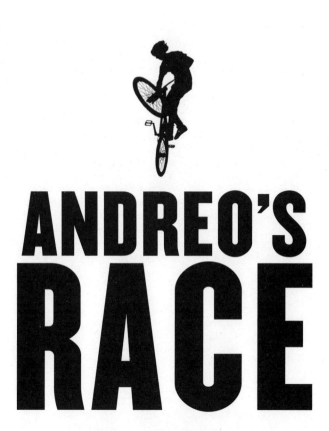

ANDREO'S RACE

Pam Withers

TUNDRA BOOKS

Published in Canada by Tundra Books,
a division of Random House of Canada Limited,
One Toronto Street, Suite 300, Toronto, Ontario M5C 2V6

Published in the United States by Tundra Books of Northern New York,
P.O. Box 1030, Plattsburgh, New York 12901

Library of Congress Control Number: 2014934267

LIBRARY AND ARCHIVES CANADA CATALOGUING IN PUBLICATION

Withers, Pam, author
Andreo's race / written by Pam Withers.

Issued in print and electronic formats.
ISBN 978-1-77049-766-5 (pbk.).—ISBN 978-1-77049-767-2 (epub)

I. Title.

PS8595.I8453A65 2015   jC813'.6   C2014-900837-6
                                      C2014-900838-4

Edited by Sue Tate
Designed by Rachel Cooper
The text was set in Van Dijck.
www.tundrabooks.com

Printed and bound in the United States of America

1 2 3 4 5 6   20 19 18 17 16 15

For my father, Richard Miller, with love

ANDREO'S RACE

CHAPTER ONE

You need the lungs and leg muscles of a giant to pump your mountain bike up a steep, twisting trail in the Canadian Rockies. Especially in pitch darkness, and even if you're drafting your hard-sweating friend Raul Jones.

It doesn't help that we've had no sleep for forty hours and the blisters on our feet are weeping yellow pus under their mummy wraps of duct tape. It doesn't help that we have another sixteen-plus kilometers (ten miles) to go. And that's assuming we're not already lost on this mountain pass. It does help that the first hints of dawn are beginning to backlight the wind-tossed trees around us.

"You still awake, Andreo?" Raul's voice bellows.

"I'm awake," I shout, blinking heavy eyelids to convince myself it's true. "I'll lead when we reach the top of this hill."

"Not." His voice drifts back to me.

In rhythm with my own haggard breathing, I work the pedals and focus on the reflective stripes of Raul's yellow bike jacket. Like glowworms, they draw me slowly up to the crest, then wrinkle and shrink as my friend raises an arm in a victory punch and speeds downhill.

I suck from my hydration pack's mouth tube and lean into my handlebars. My aching knees amp up their piston work to reach the top. Then, praying it's our last hill, I shift my weight back and lift my numb butt off the saddle, more than ready to enlist gravity for a while.

Wind numbs my ears, and my body vibrates with the effort of swerving around rocks as my bike hurtles into daybreak. After half an hour of keeping every body part flexed for shock absorption, I find myself staring wide-eyed at my friend. He's being swallowed by a blanket of fog so thick and low over the valley ahead that it feels entirely possible we're entering a zone of suffocation. It resembles a giant lake heaped with fluffy snowdrifts, but in my exhaustion, I imagine that a feathery mattress awaits, eager to embrace me, bike and all.

Instead of feathers, a cool wetness slaps my face, and visibility drops to—*Screech!* I narrowly avoid skidding into Raul. He's standing beside his bike on the side of the trail, squeezing a pack of power gel between his chapped lips.

"This fog's bad, *mon.*"

"Wrong," I reassure him. "It'll mess up the others. Not us. That's a good thing."

Raul makes a face at me. "Yeah, but we lose this trail

and we're toast. I say let's pull over. We've earned a little break. Maybe it'll thin out."

"We rest, we lose. The compass and map say we're okay. Besides, the last checkpoint should be bottom of this valley, beside the lake."

"Last checkpoint," Raul echoes, brightening. "Manned by lots of cute *chicas*, I hope." He re-straddles his bike and turns up his music. Bob Marley leaks from his earbuds through his now-bobbing dreadlocks. I grin. Sometimes I wonder if Raul thinks he's black rather than brown.

"Raul, we'll be through there so fast, we won't know if they're chicks or dudes," I say, pulling up beside him. "Remember, fog's good. Dad says I have a sixth sense when it comes to navigation. A homing instinct."

Raul removes one earbud. "Homing instinct? He means you're a pigeon-brain. But lead on, fog-man." He lifts his bony butt back onto his bike saddle and we're off.

Down into the valley we careen, wisps of fog brushing our necks. An eerie cry rises from nearby peaks. Wolves. I shudder without lifting my eyes from the trail. Most other creatures up here must be getting ready to hibernate, especially after this October cold snap. I sigh. A long winter's nap is what I need right now. I shake my head to keep myself alert.

Unlike most of the competitors in this teens-only, two-day adventure race, I've been training for this kind of event all my life. Comes with having a mother who's a former canoe racer and personal trainer, and a dad who spends every moment he's not working at his construction firm tearing around the world, competing in adventure races. Adventure races, as I'm always explaining to my eleventh-grade classmates at Canmore High, are basically multisport races in the wilderness lasting anywhere from a day or two to more than a week. It's a kind of insanity that only fitness crazies with an overload of testosterone and a need to "test their limits" go in for. Fitness freaks who also happen to have a fat wallet, since the big adventure races—not wimpy little two-day kid versions like this one—cost plenty.

That's my folks: rich, adventurous fitness fanatics. I go along with it 'cause I'm good at the navigation bit. And to fit in with my family, however hopeless *that* is. Raul does it to get away from his drunken parents.

"Yes! The lake!" I shout even before I see it. The thicker air means water is nearby, and for just a microsecond, the fog delivers the faint sound of human conversation. *Use all your senses*, Dad always says.

We ride at speed right up to some stacked crates and two folding chairs that serve as the checkpoint. Two girl volunteers from our high school smile and rise to stamp the team passport I hold out.

"Anyone ahead of us?" Raul asks the prettier of the two, even though he knows it's against the rules for them to tell.

"My lips are sealed," she replies.

"Your lips are way too pretty to be sealed. But we'll

continue this conversation later." He grins as he sprints his bike toward the mist-enshrouded beach. I follow.

"Mother!" I drop my bike and rush toward her slender, broad-shouldered form beside the lineup of canoes at the water's edge. She's wearing several fleece jackets and a lavender ski cap, black Lycra tights and brand-new, high-tech running shoes. She's not a race official here or anything, just our self-appointed trainer and fan. "Wasn't sure you'd be here."

"You've made good time," she says, studying her chronograph racing watch. "I knew you wouldn't get lost in the fog." She reaches out as if to pat my shoulder, but fails to actually touch it. Other mothers would give their son a hug, but my mother isn't the hugging kind. Not with this son, anyway. "Hurry now, boys," she urges, nodding at Raul.

Raul and I drop our packs into the nearest canoe and grab the life jackets lying inside. "Who's ahead of us?" I ask.

"Two teams," she says gravely, leaning forward to buckle my life jacket like I'm still a kid, not a sixteen-year-old. "But you're on their tail. Remember to stroke close to the canoe, let the boat glide—no lurching—and use your abdominal muscles. . . ."

"We know all that." Raul leaps into the bow and picks up the paddle lying there. "Let's go already, Team Inca."

A shadow flickers across my mother's face. She doesn't like our team name, and for a split second, I regret not vetoing Raul's suggestion. *But she'll overlook our name when we win,* I reason.

"See you at the finish!" she shouts. "There's a surprise waiting there!"

"Food, I hope," Raul says.

"David?" I contemplate, stabbing the water, then pulling with long, clean strokes.

"*Nah,* your brother's too busy at that new private school of his," Raul says.

If there's little love lost between David and me, there's a whole lot less between David and my sharp-tongued, rough-edged buddy Raul, I muse. But now's not the time to distract ourselves from hauling ass.

Bob Marley's crackly voice drifts sternward as our paddles slice through thinning mist and gray lake water.

"Fog-brain, know where we're going?" Raul asks.

"Like a laser beam."

"But Team Torpedoes is to our right, veering east."

I squint as far as the vapor will let me and detect the outline of another canoe. "That's their problem. Trust me."

Stroke, stroke, stroke. What's left of my shoulder muscles burns cruelly; my eyelids can't stay propped open much longer. Twenty minutes later, we come up on what must be the lead team's canoe. Splashes tell me that the Adventure Aces are not paddling smoothly and evenly, but hey, they didn't grow up with a mother-coach. We move into position to ride their wake. They swivel around to glare at us and unwisely pour on speed.

Fifteen minutes of piggybacking on their efforts and my nostrils smell mud and vegetation, which means we're approaching land. "Move it," I direct Raul, and we dig in to pass the would-be winners, who lack the juice now to prevent our taking the lead. Even before our canoe slides onto shore, we strip off our life jackets, let our paddles clatter to the floor and re-shoulder our packs. A startled volunteer steps forward to secure the boat.

"This is it," I shout, and up a muddy hill we charge on our last dregs of adrenaline, taking short steps and staying off the balls of our feet, just as Dad has trained us to do on steep slopes. Sunrise is finally dispersing the fog with a tangerine glow.

"*Ay yi yi!*" Raul shrieks in what he has decided is an Inca warrior cry. We grab hold of tree roots to pull ourselves over the top of the ridge and all but tumble down to the finish line. Breaking through the finish line's thin strip of orange tape feels utterly blissful. Seeing Dad leaping about and surging forward to bear-hug us both is cool. Then I spot the still figure behind him. Resentment replaces my euphoria.

"David," I say tonelessly.

"Congratulations, Andreo. First place." The voice is equally flat, almost sarcastic; the eyes narrowed. I smell jealousy and find it nourishing. I notice he has put on a slight paunch since leaving six weeks ago. Boarding-school food must be good. But before I can say anything, a burly reporter steps between us and his cameraman aims a television news camera at Raul and me. "Team Inca. How does it feel to clinch first place?"

"Awesome," I say, my legs suddenly threatening to buckle.

"And what's the secret of your success?"

"Hard training, good coaching," Dad says proudly, forgetting for a moment that it's not all about him.

"Our Inca genes," Raul says a little louder than necessary, throwing an arm around my shoulder and grinning into the camera. I watch Dad and David stiffen.

"Your Inca genes?" The newsman looks curious.

"Andreo and I are Quechua Indians, descended from the mighty Incas. We were born in Bolivia and adopted and raised by Canadian parents," Raul proclaims. "That means our lungs are descended from generations of high-mountain warriors. That's why locals here have no chance against us."

I'm too tired to roll my eyes, let alone wince on behalf of Dad, his face frozen in shock, or David, whose raised eyebrows reek of ridicule. There are two unspoken rules in our household: Never mention the *A* word and always pretend that David and I are natural brothers.

"I see," the reporter says politely.

"And you must be Nick Wilson," he says, swinging toward my dad, "a well-known adventure racer yourself. How does it feel to have your, *er*, son and his friend here place first?"

"I'm proud as hell," Dad says, averting his eyes from

Raul. "And this is my other son, David, also sixteen. . . ."

But the reporter and his cameraman have swung back to capture the Adventure Aces sprinting for the finish line.

CHAPTER TWO

"Your friend Raul could do with a little more restraint," Dad says in a friendly but measured tone from where he sits, muscle-toned and hairy-chested, across from me in the Canmore Country Club whirlpool. I look out of the tall window behind him, the one that frames a panorama of rose-colored, snowcapped peaks. I've slept all day and hauled myself out of bed just in time for this "spa and dinner night out" celebration of my adventure-race win.

"Yeah, like he's the least classy guy at Canmore High you could possibly choose to hang out with," says David as he lowers his pasty white self in baggy swim shorts into the pool in a squeeze between Mother and Dad.

Sitting across from their tight arc of three, I feel for a moment like someone being interrogated rather than celebrated.

"Raul is Raul," I state.

"Raul is a nice boy," my mother speaks up, patting

the bun into which she has wound her long dark hair to keep it dry. Her black one-piece glistens as she rises to press the power button for more Jacuzzi action. "He does well considering he's from a disadvantaged family."

"Disadvantaged?" My father scoffs as bubbles surge about us. "His folks used to be pretty well off."

Dad should know. My parents referred Raul's parents to the adoption agency that handled us both.

"Don't know how they manage to keep their jobs, though," Dad adds. "Their employer must turn a blind eye."

"Working drunks," David inserts helpfully. I feel like shoving a wall of water at him.

"Money doesn't buy happiness," my mother points out. "Anyway, Raul means well. He just has a lot of . . . ," she pauses, "spark."

"Anyone up for the steam room?" Dad asks. One by one we step out of the whirlpool, file through cold showers and enter the steam room. For an instant, I'm transported back to the early-morning fog of my race. But my sore muscles are happy for the room's searing heat.

"David, tell us more about how school is going," my mother says, her voice all but gushing. "He was placed on the honor roll already," she informs me.

I feel my jaw tighten. That would be in contrast to my all-Cs report card, with the exception of Spanish, where I managed an A minus. Truth is, like Raul, I'd way rather be outside doing something fun than inside doing homework.

"School's awesome," David says. "Teachers are way better than at Canmore High, and there are lots of clubs: Math Club, Chess Club, Current Events Club, Science Club. . . ."

"But you've left plenty of time for sports, too?" Dad asks as he stretches his body full-length on the top bench, metallic blue swim trunks sparkling in the steam. Beneath him is a fluffy white towel with a gold-threaded Canmore Country Club monogram on its corner.

"Yeah, *um*, I signed up for track, but missed the deadline, so I'll get on the team next round," David replies.

"Missed the deadline?" Dad says, rising on one elbow. He quickly lowers his voice at a signal from Mother. "Want me to talk to someone there? That was silly to get a date wrong, son, but surely they'll make an exception for you."

Missed the deadline? I wonder. He was probably too busy getting on the honor roll and beating everyone at chess. But it's true that David is a decent runner when he's training.

"And have you made friends, darling?" Mother asks.

"Yeah, I got elected student government leader," David says, his chest puffing out a little as he sits swinging his legs through the hot mist.

Power doesn't buy happiness or friends, I am tempted to say. But Mother is all smiles and pride.

"I joined the Spanish Club," I hear myself say, even though I usually avoid competing with David on anything academic.

"Yes, your Spanish is getting very good," Mother says, a little too hurriedly.

"Well," David says, standing to stretch his tall frame and tracing a line in the steam on the glass door, "people kind of expect Andreo to speak Spanish, don't they?"

I bite my lip. It's as close as David will ever come in front of Mother to referring to the difference in our skin color.

"You haven't told me yet why you're home this weekend," I address him, moving up to plop down beside Dad. *Like why you've shown up unannounced to spoil what should have been my weekend.* He has no idea how six weeks of his being at boarding school—and me having Mother and Dad to myself for the first time in my life—has given me a real taste for being an only child.

"Dad told me to come. Said he'd explain it tonight. And Mom drove all the way to the train station to pick me up." David slips his arm around her; she responds by giving him a firm hug and a peck on his cheek. I have no idea why David calls her Mom while I've always called her Mother.

Dad stands up with a grin and wraps his towel around his waist. Streamlets of hot water run down his six-pack abs. "Indeed. I have an exciting announcement to make over dinner. Shall we move to the dining room, everyone?"

Fifteen minutes later, we're seated at a table draped in white linen, intently studying oversize menus.

"I could eat a grizzly bear," I say, fully awake and ravenous now.

"And you certainly deserve anything you want on the menu, son," Dad replies.

"Including wine?" I joke.

"A sip of mine," Mother teases.

We order, clink glasses and settle back, all eyes on Dad.

"The announcement," David reminds him.

"*Ah*, yes. I have some terrific news. A brand-new international adventure race has been announced. And now that both of you have turned sixteen, I think our family is ready to do it."

"Yes!" I shout, half-jumping up from my chair. "We've done most of the U.S. and Canadian ones. About time we get to join you on a biggie."

"When? Where? What kind?" David asks.

"Yes, where?" Mother joins in. "Your father has been keeping that bit secret from me."

"It's seven-day, four-sport stage race in January—and yes, we'll arrange permission for you to miss a week and a half of school," Dad says, locking his hands behind his head and tilting back in his chair with a self-satisfied grin.

A stage race is good, I reason: mandatory breaks at intervals. Seven days flat out would be too brutal for a first international, even if David and I are way more experienced than most kids our age. And missed school time sounds like an excellent idea.

"Mountain biking, trekking, canoeing and caving," Dad elaborates.

"Caving?" David and I echo in surprise.

"Yes, that one's a bit unusual—one of those 'special feature' challenges that serves as a break from the timed portions. A Fear Factor/Wipeout sort of thing. And that's why David is home for the weekend—to do a caving certification course. He has to pass one to enter. I know yours is up-to-date, Andreo."

"Hey, Raul could coach him," I say. "Everyone knows Raul is one of the best teen cavers around." My friend is like a boa constrictor when it comes to slithering through impossibly small, dark spaces. His house just happens to be on a cave-riddled hill, and it's his other way of escaping his mom and dad.

"When I want Raul's help, I'll ask for it," David informs me.

"I've arranged some private lessons with an adult instructor before the course," Dad tells us. "But speaking of Raul, there's another issue."

I wait, hoping against hope he'll say what I want to hear.

"This race calls for teams of five, not four, including one female."

Mother smiles. She is used to being our token female, and where there's a canoeing leg, she's a female competitor most teams would kill for.

"Yes, yes, yes!" I say, jumping up again. "Raul will do it. I know he will. And he'll rock in the caving section!"

Given that adventure races can specify any number of people, I always feel lucky when they require five, allowing Raul to join us.

"I could maybe find someone from my school," David offers.

One of his many "friends" in student government? I wonder. *Or from the track team he hasn't even joined yet?* Nope, from the look on Dad's face, I know that Raul's in.

"As you know, David," Dad says, "we've run into the five-person rule twice before, and Raul has turned in impressive performances. Also, like Andreo, he speaks Spanish well, and that will be an advantage on this one."

"Spanish?" Mother says, her eyes widening. "So when are you going to tell us *where* this new race is?"

Dad's front chair legs return slowly to the floor, and he studies his table setting for a moment. Then he reaches for Mother's hand, squeezes it and says in a placid voice, almost too quietly for the rest of us to hear, "Bolivia."

I feel my heartbeat do double time, and I sit bolt upright. David shoots one narrowed-eyed glance my way and then, like Dad, studies Mother's face, which has formed a careful mask.

You see, the *B* word, being connected with the *A* word, is also banned in our household. We all pretend that I popped out of Mother here in Canada, not Bolivia, a mere six months before David—with more of a suntan, so to speak. Mother even used to call us her "twins" before she noticed that it prompted us to pummel each other.

Sure, Mother and Dad dutifully gave me the "you were adopted" talk when I was little—only after too many people had pointed out to me (meanly) that David and I couldn't possibly be "real" brothers. But, even then, I got the clear message that this information was the beginning, middle and end of the discussion.

Now, suddenly, Bolivia is real and alive and calling me. Here is a possibility I'd never even dreamed of: I can visit the land where I was born, see faces like my own— and with Raul at my side! All the while competing in our very first international race.

"Whether we go depends completely on whether you're okay with it," Dad is saying to Mother.

"But, of course," she says after a moment of studying their hands entwined in her lap. She lifts her face bravely. "It's time we did an international race together. I know you've been waiting for this for a long time, dear." She turns to meet our eyes. "And our boys are ready, aren't you, David and Andreo? Sixteen. I'm so proud of you both."

"So you're okay with where it is?" Dad presses, again his voice uncharacteristically meek.

With effort, Mother projects confident calm. "Yes, dear, we'll have a grand adventure. Now if you'll excuse me, I need to visit the powder room."

Our dinners arrive, but Dad is still watching Mother's figure disappear. David swings around to face me. "If

Raul has to come on our race, you tell him to keep his big trap shut about Inca warriors and bloodlines, you hear? It's all bullshit, anyway."

"Is it?" I say with a defiance that surprises me.

"David has a point," Dad says, staring at his food like he has lost his appetite. "Mother's sensitive. We just need to be thoughtful. I'm sure you can have a word with Raul, Andreo," he adds, meeting my eyes meaningfully.

"She's more than sensitive," David addresses me in a tone that stiffens my back. "She's fragile about this stuff and you know it. We have to protect her."

"Sensitive. Fragile," I echo, picking up my knife and fork and tearing into my steak. "Sensitive that I might run away because I'm going back to my country or something? Fragile because being there will make her remember she took me on only because she didn't know she was already expecting a real son?"

Dad, eyes flashing, leaps up and moves to tower over me. His mouth opens, but no words come out. That prompts David to raise his steak knife and jab it toward my chest. "She's the only mother we've got. Don't go hurting her or she might reject you like your last one did."

Now it's my turn to leap up, fists balled, but Dad's hands come down to clamp on our shoulders. Heedless of stares from nearby diners, he pushes us gently back into our seats and heaves a heavy sigh. "Boys, your mother and I love both of you deeply. I appreciate that you are aware of your mother's weakness and are usually very thoughtful accordingly. All I ask is that you continue to be so. And, sons, let's not spoil a dinner that is all about celebrating Andreo's impressive win today."

He returns to his seat just as Mother appears, her makeup perfectly touched up and a studied casualness in her stroll back to the table.

CHAPTER THREE

I'm swaddled in a colorful woven blanket and wearing a soft woolen baby hat on my head. I'm tucked between my birth mom and dad in the giant purple hammock that hangs between feathery green trees not unlike weeping willows. A breeze is swaying us gently, gently, and the sky is an open blue. My mom is singing a Spanish lullaby. My dad, so young and dark and handsome, is gazing into my eyes, his own alight with love. I smell coconut oil on his fingertips as they brush my cheek. I raise my chubby little baby arms to him—and he disappears. Vaporizes. Is replaced by the scent of a cigar.

The hammock shifts as my mom turns to look at an approaching stranger. He is tall and fat and faceless; there is only a blur where his eyes, nose and mouth should be. He wears a black hat and a dull gray suit with a thin green tie, and, as my mother scoops me tightly into her arms, my view is of his polished black leather shoes halting in the dirt beside the hammock. I burrow as deep as I can against my mother's chest, feeling the comforting cadence of her heartbeat. I push my face against the long black braids that spill down from her brown bowler hat, the one that smells pleasantly of wool.

But stronger arms than hers lift me up, up, up. I scream. I squirm in protest. Most of all, I try to twist around to see my mom's face. I need to see my mom's face. Has she given me up, or have I been stolen from her? I'd know if I could just see her face. And if I cry and struggle enough, surely someone will stop this from happening and save me? I open my eyes to see my adoptive mother, younger than I ever remember her, gazing down on me. Her arms are hesitant, her heart beats with an unfamiliar tempo, her eyes reveal a fleck of fear. I thrash, twist and test out the full power of my lungs.

"Andreo! Andreo! Wake up, you howling idiot. You're having your nightmare again! How do you expect anyone around here to sleep?"

Raul is standing near the foot of my bed—which is actually the spare bed in his messy bedroom. As I sit up, I recall I'm sleeping over at his house, and it's Friday night. Or more like Saturday morning, judging from the first signs of light through his droopy cotton curtains. We were planning to rise early to go caving.

"Was it the one where she gives you up or the one where you get stolen?" he asks dully, but doesn't wait for a reply. "*Mon*, you won't believe what I found on the

Internet when I googled 'Bolivia' just now. I'm printing it out for you. I was gonna wake you up, but then you started hollering."

I shift my eyes to the green glow of the computer screen on his chipped desk. High above it, dusty and forgotten, hangs a framed snapshot of his adoptive parents holding him as a baby. They are outside a white-domed building in Bolivia. I take in the whine of his printer, check my watch and leap out of bed.

"Eight o'clock?" I say. "Hey, we should be outta here. Caving, remember?"

"Yeah, yeah." He points to his backpack, stuffed and ready to go by the door. I realize he's dressed already as I race to pull on my clothes. "But this is an amazing news report. You have to read it."

"Bring it along. Let's grab some breakfast and hit the trail." We shoulder our packs and head toward the stairs. His dad appears in a rumpled bathrobe, chin grizzled and holding his head as he stumbles to the bathroom.

"Morning, Mr. Jones," I say. "Hey, thanks for giving Raul permission to do the race in Bolivia."

He stares at me and blinks. "Bolivia. Right. Anything for some peace and quiet around here." And the bathroom door slams shut.

After polishing off bowls of instant oatmeal and toast piled high with jam, we open the back door to a blast of cold air. Our boots scrunch a dusting of November snow as we head up the frozen trail.

"Not supposed to tell you this," Raul says, "but your loser brother took two tries to get his caving certificate the other weekend. As in, he flunked on his first round. A certain guide told me."

Raul wants to be a caving guide when he turns eighteen, so he hangs out with a bunch of local instructors.

"You're right, you're not supposed to tell me," I say, slapping him on the back and smiling.

My buddy pulls the Internet printout from his pants pocket. "Headline is BLACK-MARKET-BABY RINGLEADER JAILED IN BOLIVIA."

"*Huh*? Someone's jailed a baby?"

"No, stupid. Someone who sells babies illegally got caught. In Cochabamba, Bolivia. Right near where our race is going to be."

"Black babies?" I lower my pack at the cave entrance, strap on my helmet and switch on its headlamp.

"No, Andreo, babies on the black market," Raul says as we head into the dark. One by one, we grab the anchored rope, attach the aluminum hardware on our harnesses to it and make like we're firemen sliding down a pole. We land lightly in a sculpted cavern. "When rich North Americans can't find a baby to adopt, they head to places like Bolivia. They pay lotsa money—it says here fifty thousand—on the black market."

"Fifty grand?!" My voice echoes as we tramp over the stone floor, ducking under stalactites. My headlamp beam picks up bats flying overhead. "No one would pay that for me. And they'd pay a whole lot less for you."

"*Ha-ha*. But listen! This ring—these criminals—sold, like, six hundred babies over the past fifteen to twenty years, mostly to Americans and Canadians. Illegally. For the bucks. And now they've been busted. At least, the head honcho—name of Hugo Vargas—was arrested Friday."

"So?" We drop to our kneepads and crawl into a moist tunnel, Raul first as usual.

"That could be us, *mon*!" says his muffled voice. "We could be stolen goods!"

The rotten-egg smell of sulfur attacks my nostrils as we enter a bulge in the tunnel. We sit cross-legged and face-to-face in the cramped space. The packs on our backs are pressed against the walls; our heads are touching the ceiling. My beam exposes a bushy-tailed wood rat scurrying from an oversize twiggy nest down the tunnel from which we've come. "First of all, we weren't adopted illegally, Raul. At least I wasn't."

"Says who?" His voice sounds overloud in this cubbyhole, this last alcove before things get really tight in Dead End Tunnel. "You finally gonna tell me your story, or whatever fib your parents told you? Or do I guess right that your super-uptight mother has never told you anything?"

I sigh and shine my light on a sparkling droplet clinging to the end of a mud-colored stalactite. Even my best friend and fellow adoptee Raul has no idea what a huge hole in my heart exists from not knowing much else about my birth parents. For as long as I can remember, I've fantasized about finding them—maybe because I've never felt that I've fit in with my adoptive family. I've never even been sure my adoptive mother loves me. But precisely because I'm so obsessed with the issue, I'm determined to hide it from Raul. Still, maybe it's time to tell him the one stupid story I was given.

"Dad told me I was born in Cochabamba. My birth mom was a teenage beauty queen. She got herself pregnant thanks to some married doctor. Her family didn't want the scandal. The doctor—my birth father—wanted nothing to do with the whole thing." *That's why I've concocted a dream, a story I like better. Except it keeps turning into a nightmare.*

"Seriously?" His headlamp beam, frozen on my face, blinds me to his own facial expression.

I nod and glance at the coffin-size opening between slabs of rock that we've promised to tackle today. "That's what Dad told me when I was, like, twelve, and there's no way anyone in my family wants to talk about it, especially my mother, as you bloody well know. I don't want to ask questions. I don't want to get anyone's nose out of joint." I gesture to the crumpled-up printout sticking out of his pocket. "So stop digging up this shit off the Internet."

"No effing way."

I stare at Raul, who I can see now is staring bug-eyed at me. We're still sitting cross-legged in our cramped rotunda, our breaths coming out in pockets of steam. "What?"

"My parents told me the same thing. The beauty queen and doctor line!"

"Did not. You told me a whole different story."

"'Course I did! No way was I gonna 'fess up to a lame-sounding tale like that. Beauty queen? Sucky."

I shine my light on a colony of daddy longlegs on the walls. "You're not making that up?"

"You're not making up yours?"

"No." Sweating and rattled, I turn and enter the space ahead of Raul, wriggling on my stomach, hands ahead of me like I'm swimming. Raul has recently decided this isn't a dead end as the rest of the caving community believes. The reason we're here is that last weekend, he crawled in, reached the end boulder pile, hammered on it with a crowbar until he felt air flow, then shoved a few more stones away. He thinks that we, being smaller and skinnier than adult cavers, can now carry on to what may be a new exit. I'm barely in, though, when hands close over my ankles and Raul jerks me all the way back into our conference room.

"Stop, Andreo. You gotta think about this one. So both our adoptive parents got fed a line. A big sales pitch that some black-market dude thought up. It's perfect, don't you see? This baby's got beauty-queen looks and doctor brains, and no birth parents who are going to ask for it back. The perfect history. Maybe all six hundred babies he collected money for came with the same damn story."

I lean forward and blow a long breath of steam into Raul's face. "Guess that means the beauty queens in Bolivia keep pretty busy. Or maybe we have the same beauty queen mom and doctor dad, which makes us brothers." My sarcasm drips with the same ping as the stalactite's droplets.

"*Ha*! Not possible, 'cause I'm way better looking than you, not to mention I was born just four months after you."

"Drop it, Raul." I reach out and grab the printout from his pocket, shredding it with my gloved hands right in front of his eyes. "Wood-rat nesting material."

"Stop, *mon*." Raul's voice is distressed. "It said in the article that the parents who adopted kids from this baby stealer had no idea."

I stare at the pieces of paper and feel my shoulders slump. "Even if we *were* adopted illegally, it wouldn't change anything. Why hurt our parents' feelings?"

"My parents don't have feelings. And yours are way too sensitive. You have to start standing up to them, Andreo. It's your life—your history—they're hiding from you. Don't tell me you aren't curious. You with all the nightmares."

"So what if I'm curious?" I allow, ignoring the rest of his speech. "What about you? You want to find your birth parents if it's possible? You're not scared?"

He hesitates, my friend who's usually all bluff. "Yeah," he says quietly. "I want to know, I want to meet them, but another part of me doesn't want to. They could be monsters, right? Or they could be nice. Or they could be super pissed I chased them down. But this news story, this new information—how can we just ignore it? It's a sign or something."

I lean back into the hard rock wall. "Don't we have to be, like, eighteen before they let us ask for records?"

"But that's just the point. There are no records if we're black-market babies. And we're heading to Cochabamba for this race. We could poke into it while we're there." His headlamp seems to be searching my face, which has gone taut. "Without your parents knowing."

With effort, I unclench my jaw. "Let me think about it, okay? I don't want to talk about it anymore. Let's find this mystery exit you're so sure about." With that, I plunge back into the shoulder-width passage, inching forward, but I'm so distracted that I neglect to put all five senses on the alert.

Ten minutes after squeezing past the former dead end, it hits me. The air movement, the pinprick of light ahead—and the smell.

"*Eeeww*, did you just fart?" comes the muffled voice of my caving partner behind me.

I take a deep breath and have to fight a sudden need to vomit. Dead wood rat? Pile of dead wood rats? Something oily and almost overpoweringly rank, yet not the smell of death. I lift my head the three inches that the space will allow me to, my nose wrinkled to close my nostrils. I hold perfectly still, listening, breathing through my mouth, staring ahead.

"*Shhhh*," I caution Raul and reach up to flick off my headlamp. Inky blackness. Had I been imagining the light? No way. And the air movement: gone now, totally gone. Like a boulder might have rolled from somewhere to block the exit while we were talking.

Slowly, quietly, I bring my right arm up and twist it back and over my shoulder. I feel around for my trekking pole. With difficulty, I unhook it and bring it in front of my face, where I extend it and shove it ahead of me like a prod.

I move forward again, even though the crawl space is getting more constricted and airless. Anyone else would start backing up. Raul's tug on my left boot indicates that's what he thinks we should do. But my curiosity is fully aroused. There's an opening up there; I can *feel* it, even if I can't see or smell it anymore. And if it's just a stone blocking our way, then my pole, my fists and my determination will clear it.

The farther I advance, the more frantic the tugs on my boot. Raul knows it's not like me to ignore him. He's the better caver. But I'm focused on the blockage. I poke it with my pole tip, then wriggle forward to push it with my gloved hands and finally butt it with the front of my helmet. Whatever it is isn't solid. Whatever I've touched is now moving. The patch of light returns—revealing an exit to a grand cavern! Then the roaring begins, and the stench flows right through my blocked nostrils to hit me like a sewage backup.

"Bear!" I shriek, and wriggle backward so fast that one of my boots goes right into Raul's face.

"Bear?" Raul shouts, and slides backward so fast you'd think we were on a waterslide, heading feet-first on our stomachs, rather than snaking down a level passage-way. Back, back, back we scramble on elbows and knees as the hibernating creature we've disturbed settles into blocking the diminishing pinprick of light.

CHAPTER FOUR

Fat snowflakes spiraling down through evergreens land on the topographical map I have spread out on a boulder. I lay my compass on the map and memorize the location of the checkpoints. I turn my map and body in the proper direction, eye a ridge ahead and take a bearing.

"Are we lost?" David asks, but the tone isn't hard-edged or accusing. We've both been trying, this Christmas break, not to rile one another.

"Most important aspect of team racing is maintaining harmony," Dad likes to lecture us. It's an especially tall order when Raul's with us, but today it's just David and me. He and I have been trying to get in perfect shape for the race just two weeks away now, under the close supervision and training regimen of Mother and Dad. Although Raul's parents have been less than interested, they nevertheless managed to come up with the money. Between his parents and mine, we've secured special permission to miss a week and a half of school for the race and have lined up most of the gear on the race checklists.

"Nope, not lost. We're good," I say, folding the map, tucking my compass back on its wrist cord and squinting at a set of heavy gray clouds moving our way.

"What happens if you get run over by a bus and I have to play chief navigator?"

"No buses on adventure racecourses," I joke as we jog toward the ridge.

"But seriously. And what do you do if it's dark?"

"You send a teammate ahead to stand within headlamp view and take a reading on him. And you keep doing that with your teammates, using them as checkpoints to travel the plotted course."

"Right, I remember now. Figuring so many steps per kilometer."

"You got it, except they're paces, not steps. You always remember the math part."

We speed up, and I feel my blood warming.

"Remember our very first race?" David asks as we wind along the frozen dirt road.

"The obstacle course when we were seven," I reply. "The one where you hauled me to the school playground the night before and made me run it over and over in different ways while you timed me."

David's laugh is a warm, easygoing one. "Hey, I'm all about using math. But we won the next day, didn't we?"

"Tied for first. And the gold medal was—"

"A chocolate coin hung on a red, white and blue ribbon necklace," he finishes as we laugh together at the memory.

"I wanted to eat it," I say. "You wanted to wear it, and Mother had to take it away to stop us wrestling each other in the school parking lot." Of course, Mother ended up ruling that David could wear it a full day before we split it, and by then it was a melted mess. But I don't mention that, or the fact that it was one of the last races where we tied. I have always been faster than my larger, younger "brother," even if only barely.

We chat amiably, if stiffly, during half an hour's run, me slowly increasing the pace to see if I can wind him. But he seems to have whipped himself into great shape over the past weeks—which is good, I have to remind myself.

"You nervous about the Bolivian race?" he asks.

"And excited," I reply. "But it's not like we're going to do well our first international."

"I know. Dad says our goal should be to finish and that it'll be excellent experience even if we don't. A week in a warm place. It'll be awesome." He sticks his tongue out to catch flakes of snow.

"It'll be brutal," I rule, "but interesting."

We're in sight of our house now. I scan the driveway for Raul's beat-up Chevy, the one his dad crashed into a tree two weeks ago, luckily injuring nothing but the car. Not there. Instead, I see only Dad's midnight blue Jaguar pulling up.

"Mother and Dad are going to the club tonight. Want to join Raul and me for pizza?" I ask, hoping David has other plans.

"Nope, I'm off to the gym," he says, veering away and waving. "But nice run, bro. See ya later."

Bro? Definitely not a David word.

"Okay, see ya, bro," I reply with just a hint of sarcasm.

"Andreo. Good run?" Dad asks, walking into the house with stacks of what look like store-wrapped Christmas presents.

"Yup," I say. "David kept up."

"Good man," Dad says, dumping the packages on the marble kitchen counter and pulling a manila envelope out of his coat pocket.

"Guess what I've got," he says as he strides over to the large Canadian Rockies oil painting that hangs over our new leather living-room sofa set.

"Passports?" I guess.

"Yes, Raul's too, from his parents. And the flight info. Help me with the painting?" I nod and grab the bottom edge of the frame opposite to the one he's gripping, and we slide it on its hidden railings to reveal the family safe. He hesitates as he lifts his hand to the keypad lock. "Make us some coffee, son?"

I knew he'd find a smooth way to make me turn my back as he punched in the keypad buttons. I've never in my life been allowed to see him or Mother opening that safe. Nor, as far as I know, has David.

"Coffee coming up." I head to the kitchen.

I hear the creak of the safe's door hinges and turn to watch him stash the passports and Bolivia flight information inside. I also see a plastic bag fall out. Dad dives to retrieve it, only to have his foot accidentally send it shooting across the polished hardwood floor. I walk over and pick it up. When I straighten up, I see his hands extended for it, his eyes avoiding mine.

For some strange reason, instead of handing it over, I reach inside the bag. I pull out a hand-knitted baby cap that is a riot of colors. The pinks, greens, yellows and blues are all but psychedelic in brightness. They march around the tiny bonnet in geometric patterns, the wool as soft as I imagine a baby lamb or llama would feel. Fluffy tassels hang from each side, and a multicolored braid trims the edge. I may know nothing about knitting, but I can tell it's the work of someone very skilled. It can have been created only for a baby, and I don't need to search my father's guilty eyes to know my birth mother knitted it for me.

My birth mother: the taboo subject. Is it because it's taboo that I've spent so much of my life wondering about her? Neither of us speaks as the grandfather clock ticks loudly in the corner of the room.

"Mine?" I finally manage to ask.

He nods.

"I was wearing it when you, *um*, got me. And you saved it."

He nods again.

"But you've never shown it to me before."

Dad looks around as if checking to see that my mother isn't home. "We were going to give it to you one day."

A thousand questions pour into my mind like they're being fed through a pressurized fire-hydrant hose. *Did you meet her? What did she look like? Why did she give me away? What about my father? What else in the safe is mine? And why is Mother so uptight about me being adopted? Why is she—the word occurs to me for the first time—almost* scared *of me?*

But no words spill out. We're still staring at one another as I realize I've pressed the baby hat to my nose. It smells like . . . wool. What did I expect?

Dad's hands lift again to collect it. A mix of tenderness and sympathy has replaced the guilt in his eyes now. Maybe he's flashing back to his first sight of me as a baby, me wearing it. I shake my head vigorously at him and tuck the cap under my arm, furious at myself for the lock on my tongue, yet fearful that one more word out of me will remove the tenderness in his eyes, will shut down any chance of continuing this conversation someday, will irretrievably alter the loving relationship I have with him.

They're the only family you've got. Don't go hurting them, or they might reject you like your last one did. A version of David's words, accompanied by a crushing fear I didn't know I had within me, squeezes my brain like the onset of a migraine.

I jump as the metal safe clangs shut. So he's going to

let me keep it. Wordlessly, we slide the picture back into place. I jump again as Raul's voice calls out from the kitchen. "Anyone home? I'm starving for pizza."

As my friend strolls into the living room, Dad grins at Raul innocently. "Just on my way out, Raul. Meeting Pearl at the club." He pulls his wallet out of his dress-pants pocket and lays two crisp twenty-dollar bills on the kitchen counter: way more than we need. *Guilt money?* "You two enjoy your pizza, and we'll see you later. Just two weeks till the adventure race, boys. Bet you can hardly wait."

Neither Raul nor I moves to touch the money after the back door slams shut. I notice the coffee Dad asked for is dripping. I pick up the phone to order our usual pizza. By the time I click off, my suspicions about the way Raul is looking at me are too strong to ignore.

"How long have you been in the kitchen?"

"Long enough to see what code he punched in."

I narrow my eyes and glance involuntarily at the picture.

"Nice hat," he adds. I jam it into my tracksuit pants pocket and refuse to answer.

"It's yours." He looks out the window behind him to ensure the Jag is gone. "And there's gotta be more stuff in there that's yours," he says more forcefully as he marches to the picture. "Help me roll back the picture, Andreo. We need whatever else is in there before we hit Bolivia."

I hesitate, and turn. "It's actually none of your business." He's got hold of one corner of the picture frame, and he's struggling to slide it.

"You're going to wreck the—" I lurch over to grab the other corner, meaning to resist his push, but somehow the picture slides easily and Raul, dirty boots and all, steps onto our leather sofa to punch in numbers. I can't believe he's doing this. I'm half-panicked by the notion that Dad or David or Mother will walk in. But instead of tackling my friend, I stand there watching as the safe door swings open once more.

I know I should be telling him off, but a curious feeling of elation takes over. Access at last to the family safe, where secrets about my birth parents may be hiding. Secrets I've yearned to uncover all my life. So why am I shaking, unable to reach in for them?

With one sweep of his arm, Raul pushes the entire contents of the safe onto the sofa, then steps down and looks at me—flushed, triumphant, defiant.

"Take your boots off," I order him. While he's doing that, I sit down and begin going through the pile of documents. Mortgage stuff, Mother's and Dad's and David's birth certificates, insurance papers, the passports and Bolivia trip information. We toss it all aside, pawing ever more desperately through the paperwork.

"Got it," I say in a husky voice, lifting a yellowed envelope with "*Documentos de adopción*" in large black type.

I spill the contents onto my lap. An aged photo catches

my eye first: Mother and Dad standing in front of a domed, whitewashed stucco building on a cobbled street. They seem very young. Mother is clutching a small baby wrapped in a woven blanket. She's smiling glowingly at the camera. I can just spot the knitted cap on my head. Dad, his arm slung around her, looks proud and protective.

"I've never seen this photo before."

"There's a man behind them," Raul says.

I move the photo closer to examine the shadowed doorway of the domed building. Yes, there's a tall fat man in a black felt hat and a cheap business suit standing there. He's holding something to his face—a cigar, perhaps. Or maybe he's just moving his hand to his face to cover it. Either way, his action at the moment of the click blurs his features.

I return my eyes to my parents. They look happy.

Raul grabs the papers. My hand closes over his wrist as he waves three forms in the air.

"*Certificado de Nacimiento*—that's the birth certificate," he says.

"Certification of Birth Abroad and Order of Adoption," I read out the titles of the other two.

"Order of Adoption? What's that? I've never gotten that off my parents," Raul says.

I shrug and scan the birth certificate first. There's a big official circular stamp in the middle. "Born in Cochabamba. Male. Mother: Vanessa Gutierrez. And my birth date." I pause. "Hey, my real last name is Gutierrez." I brush my fingers over her signature and try to picture her.

I remember Raul showing me his birth certificate once. It listed his birth mother as Adriana Apaza and his father as "unknown."

Raul leans over my birth certificate. "Father: unknown." He frowns. "We'll find him too, Andreo. And mine."

I gather up the contents of the precious envelope in my arms. "We're not necessarily chasing anyone down in Bolivia," I say. "All I've agreed to do is go to a library or city hall or something to see if there's more information. Only if there's time and if my parents never, ever find out."

Raul looks like he's going to argue, but holds his tongue.

"Stand guard at the window while I go photocopy these in Dad's office." I glance nervously at the wall painting and wide-open, empty safe.

Dad's printer is spitting out the final page—the Order of Adoption—when I notice one of the signatures at the bottom: Hugo Vargas. The guy in the Internet article Raul found, the black-market Bolivian arrested for selling babies.

"Raul!" I call out.

But his own shout drowns out mine: "Someone's here!"

To the sound of a car motor in the driveway, we jam everything back into the safe, including the yellowed envelope whose contents I've now copied and stuffed in my shirt. We slam the safe door shut and roll the painting back in place. Then Raul walks slowly to the door.

I hear his elated voice: "Pizza's here!"

CHAPTER FIVE

More than a dozen mountain bikes in boxes or cases are advancing toward us by forklift across the airport tarmac. We nod at what look like fellow adventure racers newly arrived from around the world as we sit beside piles of shrink-wrapped backpacks to which helmets, trekking poles, sleeping pads and canoe paddles are strapped.

The five of us—excited and eager to stretch our legs after several long flights—gaze about the modern, spacious airport in Cochabamba, trying to believe that we're really here.

"Okay, as soon as we've got our bike cases," Dad begins, "we catch a minibus taxi to our hotel and rest up. We've got one free day to get used to this elevation, so take it easy today."

"Wish they'd let us know the route before the first day of the race," I say, eager to pore over maps and start strategizing.

"But that's part of the fun, not knowing," says David.

I take out my binoculars and compass. "Bolivia has tons of national parks. Southeast of us is Torotoro National Park, with some crazy canyons and caves. I'm thinking the caving bit might be held there." I turn and point east. "Somewhere that way is Carrasco National Park; maybe one of the sports in the racecourse will go through there. Plus there are two other giant national parks north and east of it." As I face northeast, a spectacular snow-covered peak winks at me in the bright sun. "And that's Mt. Tunari."

"Love this springlike weather," my mother says, gazing about at the rolling, sparsely vegetated hills, one with a massive Christ statue with outstretched arms.

"Spring weather to us, but it's the rainy season here," Raul reminds her.

"I'm okay with sun in the rainy season," David says as the forklifts arrive and he steps forward to claim his fancy new mountain-bike case. "Good thing they're supplying the canoes. Must've cost a fortune to bring our bikes."

"It did, but never mind," says Dad. "Now, team, I'm passing each of you some money to stash in your money belts. Feel free to use it for the occasional souvenir or snack, but most of it's for emergencies, remember."

"Can I go flag down a minibus?" Raul asks. "Can't wait to use my Spanish."

Dad and Mother nod approval, but I notice that Raul's

path to the taxi lineup takes him on a zigzag route from one hot Hispanic girl to another. A few indulge him in conversation practice.

Half an hour later, we've barely checked into our rooms at one of the city's few five-star hotels when Dad, Mother and David announce they're off to the palm-treed courtyard's mosaic swimming pool "to get used to this elevation."

"Not us," Raul says before I can open my mouth. "Andreo and I were born at this elevation, and we're hitting the market now."

My family members exchange glances, but no one's in a mood to argue. "All the more room in the pool for us," David says.

With that, we're off, free to race fleet-footed through the narrow and sometimes cobbled streets of this city of almost a million. We pass squares with flowers and grass, and a stately building with a clock tower and walkway under stone arches. We dodge dusty buses, men in colorful striped ponchos and women carrying babies in richly woven slings. Vendors call out, trying to sell us bright baskets, hats, purses and fabrics.

Back at the airport, people had stared at us, clearly knowing we were foreigners. They were the kind of stares I've had to deal with all my life in a community of few Hispanic people, the type of stares my parents learned to ignore long ago when out with their two young sons: one brown, one white.

But without my parents and David, I find that no one gives us a second glance, not even at Raul with his dreadlocks. It's a heady feeling, this blending in for the first time in my life. Or maybe it's the altitude's effect—2,548 meters, or over 8,000 feet—making me light-headed. When we find ourselves in a market featuring delicious-smelling food, I say, "Hold up, Raul."

"Yeah, *mon*, I'm starved too," he says.

"*¿Qué es eso?*" we try out in Spanish, stopping before an indigenous man with meat on a stick over a hot grill. *What is that?*

"Guinea pig," he replies in Spanish. Raul and I wrinkle our noses, then grin and produce some coins.

"When in Bolivia, eat like Bolivians," I say. Guinea pig turns out to be delicious.

The vendor, obviously noticing that our accents don't match our Quechuan faces, studies us curiously. "Quechuan?" he asks.

"Quechuan Canadian," I reply politely as we move toward a fruit stand. There, we buy bananas from a kind-looking woman in a broad white straw hat, hoop earrings, plastic sandals and a checked apron. I hold up my photo of the domed building and ask if she knows where it is. She points down a street and gives me a stream of directions I can barely follow.

"*Gracias!*" we say—*thank you*—and are off again, walking now to accommodate our full stomachs.

"There it is!" I say finally. My stomach goes tight and

my breathing becomes shallow. The domed building is in greater disrepair than in the photos, its paint faded and peeling. Three beggar girls about our age are sitting on its steps, barefoot and filthy, in sacklike dresses. I offer one my banana, which she grabs and peels as she mumbles timid thanks.

Just then, a tall fat man in a business suit and shiny black leather shoes emerges from the building. "Go! No food here!" he says to them in Spanish as they flee to a nearby alley.

"Nuisances," he says, fingering a thin mustache and tipping his broad-brimmed black felt fedora at us in apology before strolling down the street. I turn to see the girls pause and peer back at us. As a breeze rustles their dresses, I realize that all three are pregnant.

"That fat man reminds me of someone," I say.

But Raul has leapt up the steps and is examining a plaque. "It's an office building," he says. We run our fingers down the list of business names.

"Hugo Vargas," I say gravely, the first to see it. We look at one another, and I push open the heavy wooden door.

"Wait, Andreo, what's our plan?"

"Plan? Who needs a plan? The guy's in jail anyway. Maybe there's a secretary with files that would help us."

"Yeah, right," Raul says. "A guy who sold six hundred babies on the black market and got locked up for it is going to have all the up-to-date addresses of the moms who gave us away, ready for a pretty secretary to hand out to anyone who wanders in."

I turn and face my friend. "Raul, now that we're here, we have to at least see the place and play things by ear."

"True," he agrees, glancing about. "Okay, boss. Onward."

Up the worn marble steps we go, our footfalls echoing in the skylight-illuminated grand stairwell. Our hands slide along its wrought-iron railings. Up to Office 13. We pause, crushed. The door is open and the room is bare. Electrical wires poke out from the walls and ceiling. Dust covers everything. We walk in, worn floorboards creaking with each step. I rest my hand on a broken electric fan. "Oh, well."

"Good afternoon. May I help you?" booms a voice in Spanish in the doorway. A short, trim bald man in a pinstriped suit is beaming at us as if he delights in visitors. A waft of his cologne drifts our way.

"*Um*, just looking around. Leaving now," Raul says in nervous-sounding Spanish.

"You have a connection with Hugo Vargas?" the man asks in perfect English, looking us over closely but without losing his smile.

"Sort of," I blurt, with a sidelong glance at Raul.

"Yes," Raul declares, studying the man intently.

"Maybe I can help you," he replies, extending his hand. "Diego Colque, from the office next door. Private detective. Coffee in my office? Bolivia makes the best in the world, you know."

Since I can't come up with a reason not to, and since fresh-brewed coffee suddenly sounds very appealing, we follow him into his carpeted office next door, past the DIEGO COLQUE: DETECTIVE PRIVADO plate on the door. He gestures for us to pull upholstered chairs up to his massive mahogany desk, which is piled with papers. The window behind him frames the snow-covered peak overlooking the city.

"You are possibly adoptees handled by Señor Vargas?" he asks. I hear myself draw in my breath. Raul's jaw comes unhinged.

"P-p-possibly," I reply, my hand automatically moving to the photocopied adoption document signed by Vargas in my jeans pocket. I steal a look at Raul, whose face is struggling to project confidence, but whose hands are pressed so tightly together in his lap, they've turned white.

"Well, as you may or may not be aware, Bolivian police have developed an interest in Señor Vargas and his adoption agency, which was recently shut down. I am working with police to analyze his files, gather information and locate both his former clients and him."

"Locate him?" Raul barks. "I thought he was in jail."

"Arrested recently, yes, but there was insufficient evidence to hold him. So he was released on bail, and now he has disappeared. I rented this office beside his old one specifically to help people like you. As we continue building our case, we are confident he will be rearrested and tried. Tell me, was one or both of you adopted? Can you furnish me with appropriate dates and information?"

"We don't have any money to pay you," I say, wiping sweat from where it threatens to dribble down my forehead.

"But that is not a problem," Detective Colque replies. "It is the police department that pays my salary on this case. Also, I am finding it very fulfilling to help match adoptees with their birth parents—where that is possible and if that is what they desire."

"We're only sixteen," Raul says, frowning. "Don't you need our adoptive parents' permission?"

The detective tilts back his padded leather swivel chair, rests his hands behind his shiny head and grins. "If Señor Vargas had done things in accordance with the law, it would be absolutely true." The chair drops back to level, and he stabs his pen at a stack of file folders on his desk. "But, sadly, that was not the case with this criminal, and I mean to make him suffer for it. But, speaking of your adoptive parents, might they be willing to supply me with information, perhaps sign a document on how Señor Vargas went about his business with them?"

"No way!" I reply with more vigor than I intended.

Raul and I chat with Detective Colque for half an hour, me showing him my papers, which he photocopies and hands back, and Raul relating his own birth certificate details. As we relax and the conversation flows, I begin to feel an enormous relief—like a shaken-up can of pop whose lid has just come off. A lifetime of hopes, fears and emotions are spilling into the room. Ignoring Raul's raised eyebrows, I even share bits of my dreams. Detective Colque nods and takes notes, his kindly face calm and encouraging, as if he has heard it all before.

"I can help," he assures me. "I love helping. So you, Raul, don't have your Order of Adoption. It means we can't be sure Señor Vargas handled your case. But given your birth date and the fact you were born in Cochabamba, I may be able to help, young man—if you'd like me to try."

"Sure," Raul says after a moment's hesitation, "even though my birth parents will probably end up being worse than my adoptive ones."

Detective Colque offers Raul a curious but sympathetic look. "It's true that adoptees have to be prepared for possible disappointment," he says gently.

Then he turns to me. "Now, you two are off on this adventure race, and you have no cell phone, but perhaps I can send you updates by e-mail? Where does your race route take you?"

"We don't know that until race day," Raul informs him.

"Really? That's interesting. Well, there are Internet cafés in most villages in Bolivia."

Ten minutes later, we're flying down the staircase, whooping and high-fiving as we burst through the front door.

"So easy," I marvel. "We might actually find out whether our birth parents are still alive and why they gave us up. That's all I want."

"Not to meet them?"

"No," I lie as an image of my adoptive mother's face flashes into my mind. If she knew we were here. . . . A knot of guilt forms in my throat, momentarily choking the excitement.

"Well, he may not actually find out anything, especially in my case—thanks to my adoptive parents not having saved all the paperwork."

I feel a stab of guilt at Raul's tone of resignation and resentment.

"Maybe that won't make any difference," I say, resting my hand on his shoulder.

Truth is, I'm feeling so hopeful that I'm almost lightheaded, but given the shadow on Raul's face, I decide it's time to change the subject. "Okay, it's all about the adventure race now," I say cheerfully.

Raul nods. "Speaking of which, the last one to the hotel hot tub is a slacker," he says. We all but knock down a dozen Cochabamba residents as we dart through the crowds back to our hotel.

CHAPTER SIX

David, Raul and I are cruising the streets of Cochabamba, being tourists in the warmth and sunshine, when I sense we're being followed. Twice I whirl around to the sound of bare feet padding on the pavement behind us, but whoever is in pursuit seems to hide in time. Finally, I catch sight of them: the three beggar girls in their over-size raggedy dresses.

"Guys," I inform my companions as we step into a cobbled alleyway between two-story stucco buildings. "Don't look now, but we're being tailed."

"And we're in a dead-end alley," David observes, turning and removing his hands from his pockets as if ready for a fight. Raul and I spin slowly, only to see a slim woman of about thirty standing in the center of the lane. She has two long, thick, black braids and sparkling red earrings that set off her sun-reddened cheeks. She's wearing a white blouse and gathered cotton skirt: black with embroidered red and white stripes near the hem. A colorful striped poncho rests over her narrow shoulders, and dainty sandals protect her feet from the cobbled street. A brown bowler hat perches on her head. She's startlingly attractive for her age. Her eyes are on me.

"Detective Colque told me you're looking for me," she says in accented English.

I feel my skin prickle. I exchange glances with Raul.

"You look just like I expected," she says, moving forward and beaming. "Handsome and strong-built, like your dad. Sixteen now, right?"

"Who is this woman?" David asks, his voice cracking.

She holds open her arms; bracelets on her wrists jingle musically. "Andreo, my son, we finally meet."

I move toward her, drawn as if in a dream, when three men appear behind her, grab her roughly and drag her backward. One, the mustached fat man with the black fedora I saw earlier, clamps a hand over her mouth and turns to glare menacingly at me.

"You! Leave her alone, you hear? Or you'll be sorry . . ."

"Mom!" I shout. I try to sprint forward, but both David's and Raul's hands grab on to my elbows. "Mom! Someone! Help!"

From above, a woman opens a window and empties a bucket of water into the lane, striking me full force in the face.

"Mom!" I shout, struggling more violently against my companions' restraint.

———

"Andreo, I'm here," I hear my adoptive mother's voice. "Are you okay? You're having a nightmare. David, it was quite unnecessary to toss a glass of water in his face."

I sit up in my hotel bed to see Mother in her night-gown perched by my side, David in pajamas holding an empty water glass and Raul behind them peering sympathetically at me. I wipe droplets of water from my face and blink at the trio.

"Oh."

"Way to wake up half the hotel," David says. "Like we need to kick off the race in a few hours exhausted from your ranting."

"Do you think you can get back to sleep now?" my mother asks, touching my shoulder gently.

I know I'm too old for a motherly hug following a disturbing nightmare, especially in front of David and Raul, but for a split second, that's what I long for. And yet, even when I was little, I don't remember her doing that. Just the light, tentative touch on the shoulder. *Does she know what my nightmares are about?*

I flop back down, turn my head to the wall and growl, "Thanks for the shower, David. And you can turn off the light now. Sorry."

The door clicks as Mother leaves; David and Raul crawl back into their beds. When I hear both breathing deeply, I rise, pull on my clothes and tiptoe down a narrow stairwell. In the lobby, a sleepy attendant observes me blandly as I seat myself at the Internet terminal.

Sure enough, an e-mail from Detective Colque.

Andreo, I've been able to confirm that your
birth mother was born in a small village near
Cochabamba. She moved to Cochabamba at the
age of seventeen, after being rejected and
shunned by her family. She gave birth to you
here, then seems to have disappeared. So far,
I've found no death certificate, so she is
likely still alive. Nor marriage certificate,
though I am still searching, as that would
give us a different name to pursue.

I will update you and Raul (on whom I've
found nothing so far) as I can. When does
your race start, and where will it take you?
Good luck, and please contact me should you
come across any helpful information yourself.

Sincerely, Detective Diego Colque

I sigh. "Well, that's something."

After hesitating for a moment, I type Thanks, but
what small village near Cochabamba? P.S. We won't
know our race route till later this morning.
Then I traipse back to bed and sleep soundly until my
alarm goes.

Three large buses with plush seats move from hotel to
hotel until all twenty-five teams of five are aboard,

motoring northeast out of Cochabamba to the mystery starting point. Partway up a paved road with heavy truck and bus traffic, we're discharged into a giant parking lot where minibuses full of our bikes—collected from us earlier—are waiting. More excitingly, we're issued maps of the region, checkpoints marked carefully. Dad allows me to spread these out as the rest of our group looks over my shoulders.

"So, our first leg is biking," Dad declares, his eyes sparkling as he moves in his sleek, black Lycra bike gear to claim our bikes. At one end of the parking lot, a giant banner is strung between two poles: COCHABAMBA ADVENTURE RACE it declares above a podium on which three officials with microphones and a couple of media types await us. According to announcements being made, the first is the mayor of Cochabamba, the second the race organizer and the third a police official who will advise us on traffic safety for biking on this crazy road. Barely into the speeches, it's this third guy—a tall, straight-backed man in police uniform—who takes long strides toward us, followed by a knockout cute, athletic-looking teenage girl.

"Team Family Dynamics, I presume?" He addresses us in clear English, his face and tone friendly. It's the lame team name Dad came up with after commenting that "Raul is honorary family for the week." Dad invited no further opinions on the matter.

"Yes, that's us," Mother says, looking slightly alarmed.

"Ricardo Ferreira, Cochabamba police chief," he says, extending his hand. Mother and Dad shake it nervously as he looks at David, Raul and me. The three of us, of course, are staring at the girl. What guy wouldn't?

"It turns out your team has the youngest competitors, along with Maria here from Team Cochabamba. So the mayor would like to get you kids up on the podium for photos and our little send-off celebration, if you don't mind."

We nod at Maria and follow the police chief. Photographers shoot us as Raul tries to impress Maria with his Spanish and teams gather around the podium to hear the race organizer's speech.

We're reminded of a bunch of rules we know already: no phones or electronic devices allowed, so no one can use them to cheat. The five members of each team must stay within sight of each other at all times. Teams get a special booklet called a team passport, which must be stamped at the checkpoints stationed every fifty kilometers (thirty miles) or so. Teams must halt at two designated stopping points—one overnight and the other a full day's rest. Their check-in and check-out passport stamps will prove they've done so. Each team has been given a satellite phone in a sealed bag, to be used for emergencies only. We can get disqualified for breaking the phone seal or using a GPS device, and there are time penalties for going out-of-bounds. And finally, if anyone drops out, the rest of the team can continue but will move from a "ranked" to an "unranked" category (which is better than the third option, the "did not finish" category).

"Remember, Family Dynamics," Dad says in a low voice after the speech, "it's our first international, so the goal is just to finish. But I'm betting we're good enough that we won't finish last."

Twenty minutes later, we're on our bikes, the starting gun goes off and under the gray morning sky, 125 cyclists—twenty-five teams of five—hit the potholed highway that rises steadily toward the heavens.

Maria's team, which includes her dad and three uncles, is pumping alongside ours, just behind the middle of the pack. "So what's your specialty?" I ask her after we introduce ourselves. "Biking, trekking, canoeing . . . ?"

"Caving," she answers confidently. "But I'm getting better at the rest. What about you?"

"Biking and navigation," I say. "My mother's awesome at canoeing, my dad is—"

"An ace at everything," David finishes for me. "I'm David, Andreo's brother, and those are our parents."

David is competent but not special at anything, except at being Mother and Dad's favorite, I want to say.

"Your parents?" Maria's eyebrows rise as she looks from David to me. The skin color difference, of course.

"I'm adopted," I explain, "like my friend Raul here. We were born in Cochabamba."

"Really?" she says. "My dad is Australian; he married my mom here."

"That explains your perfect English," David says, trying out a deep voice that sounds ridiculously fake.

"Did you say you're a caver?" Raul asks breathlessly as he noses his bike up between Maria and me. "I'm totally into caving too."

"Cool," she says.

As Mother and Dad chat with Maria's dad and her Hispanic uncles, the ever-spreading-out pack of cyclists rises into a humid fog on a narrow, winding highway. Trucks and buses blast their horns at us and spatter gravel in our faces. Rarely stopping, we press on, occasionally sucking liquid from our hydration pack tubes or shoving an energy bar into our mouths. Our legs burn and our hips grow stiff, but months of training have put us in decent shape, and the thrill of being part of Day One almost counteracts the squeeze that the elevation exerts on our lungs.

Checkpoint No. 1 turns out to be a rickety table manned by a row of serious-faced men in baseball caps and bright red-and-blue ponchos. We dismount long enough to walk around and rub our sore muscles. Dad dictates a fifteen-minute break; Raul, David and I are happy that Maria's group does the same.

"Wonder where the front cyclists are," Dad mumbles around a sandwich.

"Wonder how many teams will finish," Mother

comments as we watch someone walk his bike up to the checkpoint, then break out a tire repair kit.

"Pacing is the key," David affirms.

"For sure, especially with teenagers." Maria's dad, who introduces himself as Ethan McLeod, addresses Dad.

"Are we going to bike all night long, Dad?" David asks.

I check my map. "It's a hundred and sixty kilometers—a hundred miles—from Cochabamba to a village called Villa Tunari, but we got dropped partway up this stretch. Once we reach the highest point, Checkpoint No. 2, it'll be . . ."

". . . a terrible road and lots of downhill on the way to Villa Tunari, which is in the rain forest, not far from the jungle," Maria informs us with a smile.

"What's the difference between rain forest and jungle?" David asks.

"Rain forest is at a slightly higher elevation than jungle—it's cool, and the jungle is hot, so there are different kinds of animals and plants and stuff," she replies. "Villa Tunari is where Checkpoint No. 3 is—and the first required break."

"Sketchy to bike this highway in the dark," I observe as a truck packed with ears of corn rattles past, barely bothering to veer around some cyclists, who raise their fists in response. "And it's getting cold."

"We'll break for three hours' sleep on the side of the highway at some point," Dad rules. "Maybe around Checkpoint No. 2."

"Sounds like a plan," Maria's dad comments. "Want to ride together, draft each other if that works?"

"Sure," Dad says.

"The info sheet says we get to stay in dormitories at Villa Tunari," Mother says wistfully. "I'm hoping for hot showers, a nice restaurant meal and a sleep-in."

"We could use all of those for sure, *mon*," Raul mumbles.

Personally, I'm hoping for an Internet café.

"Okay, break's up. Ready, Maria?" Raul stands and fetches her bike for her like he's some kind of newly hired servant.

"Come on, team," David says, frowning at Raul's back. "Only six and a half days to go . . ."

CHAPTER SEVEN

Every muscle in my body is sore after the almost-twenty-four-hour ride. And it's not as if sleeping in a cold ditch on the mountain, with vehicles hurtling by, was very restful. But it's noticeably warmer here in Villa Tunari, with a steady rainfall. A short designated rest in an actual bed so early in the game feels amazing.

I wake before the others and sneak out of our dormitory to find the Internet café.

Dear Andreo: Since my last e-mail, I've been able to determine that her parents have passed away, and no one has any idea who her boyfriend—in other words, your father—was. She has had no contact with family members since she left at seventeen, and they have made it clear they want nothing more to do with her or my investigation, since she "shamed" them. Let me know where you are now and where

you'll go next. I admire your family's energy
and dedication to adventure racing.

  Sincerely, Detective Colque

I type a brief reply outlining our race route and telling him about the long ride to Villa Tunari. Maybe I
can make some more inquiries on our next break,
in Torotoro, I suggest.

By the time I return to the dormitory, everyone has
left to go see some nearby wildlife rescue center—
everyone except Mother.

"Oh, Andreo, there you are. We wondered where you'd
gone. Would you like to have breakfast together?"

"Sure. I was just wandering around the village."

We stroll down the uneven paved streets between
concrete shacks with red-tiled roofs and a few hotels and
cafés, avoiding a stray pack of scruffy dogs. Men and
boys in jeans are loading boxes into a rusty pickup truck.
Nearby, a baby sleeps beside a pile of tomatoes and
cucumbers that her mother, shawl pulled tightly around
her, is selling from a low stool on the sidewalk.

"It's exciting, racing here as a family," Mother says
as a waitress pours her coffee moments later.

"Yup," I reply. "What was it like being in Cochabamba
again?"

Her hand tightens on her coffee cup at the word "again."

"It's a bit of a crowded, dirty city. But a nice tempera-
ture. Did you like it?"

"Has it changed much?"

Her eyes meet mine with difficulty. I try to insert the person across the table from me into the photo of the happy couple clutching the new baby wearing the cap that they've hidden away from me ever since—the cap tucked this very moment into my backpack. She has gone quiet as she pokes at her egg on toast.

"Did you ever meet her?" I ask in a husky voice, lifting my coffee to my lips, only to scald them.

"No," she finally replies in a tight whisper, shaking her head vigorously. She takes a long sip from her cup. "You were a beautiful baby," she finally says, eyes lifting to mine once again. "Even if you did cry a lot. And we have been so privileged to have you."

Silence stretches between us. Again, questions shoot up from somewhere in my chest but get blocked in my throat. Mother's eyes are tearing up, something so rare that I find myself staring.

"More coffee?" Mother asks the waitress. Then she seems to concentrate on pulling herself together. "Maria's a nice girl, isn't she?"

I shrug noncommittally.

"Her dad says she's taking modeling courses. She even won a beauty queen contest last month. That's a big thing in South America, I understand."

Beauty queen. Like my birth mother? *Nah*, that was a made-up story.

"Andreo? You seem to be daydreaming. It was quite a

ride to here, wasn't it? Dry, then forest, then jungle. Sticky, then foggy, then cool, now warm." She smiles. "But we made it. And that was a good idea David had, us taking turns with the bungee cord."

"Maybe," I allow reluctantly. At the time, I'd been furious when David had whipped out the bungee cord we always carry and suggested we take turns connecting up: the stronger and more alert guiding those who were temporarily sagging. Tired as I was at the time, I felt humiliated to be half-towed by Dad at one point. Looking back, I know now it was key to getting us here without further rest stops.

"David's doing very well, considering he was so focused on studies this fall. He did us proud, getting into that school."

Us? Trust her to start in praising her precious David, when he's clearly the weak link in our team here.

"You know, he has become very interested in navigation," she continues. "You could help him with that."

That's David, always eager to muscle in on my territory. "Maybe," I reply vaguely, then stand up. "Mother, meet you at the shuttle buses in a few minutes. Gotta do something quick." Ignoring her look of surprise, I sprint to the Internet café.

Andreo: You're going to Torotoro? Good for you! I hope you manage the challenging trek from Villa Tunari to the lake okay. Again,

I'm working hard on things and will update you
soon. E-mail me when you can.

  Detective Colque

I don't bother replying. I'm suddenly on another mission. I type "Vanessa Gutierrez" and "beauty queen" into a search engine. Up come a black-and-white photo of a teenage girl and the date of the pageant: a year before my birthday. VANESSA GUTIERREZ OF TOROTORO, says the caption.

"Torotoro?" I almost shout in excitement. Detective Colque had said *a small village near Cochabamba*. He was right! I press PRINT and exit hurriedly from the screen as David stomps into the room.

"Shuttle buses are here already, you idiot. You going to wreck this race for us? What's with the sudden Internet fixation? You have a girl at home or something?"

I say nothing, pay at the front desk and head toward the door, two paces behind him. I pause just long enough to reach for the page from the printer, but David's too fast for me. It tears in half as he grabs it from my hand.

"*Ooh*, we do have a girl. Wait'll I tell Mom and Dad."

My teeth practically crack as I grit them to stop myself from answering.

The morning's start point, as it turns out, is on the far side of a wide, raging river, at which the buses leave us. In the drizzle, word spreads that we get to cross it by cable car. In the lineup, I notice that Raul is looking grumpy.

"Your brother is a swine," he hisses in my ear.

"That's news?"

"He's hanging all over Maria."

"Boys, keep the line moving, please," says Mother from directly behind us. I'm guessing she has overheard.

David manages to squeeze into a cable car beside Maria, who is all but ignoring him. Raul glowers but misses a chance to push his way aboard. I turn and notice Maria's dad and uncles keeping a hawk's eye on the beauty-queen caver.

On the far side of the river, we line up near a statue of a young man pointing down the trail.

"MARCELO QUISPE," I read. "TRAIL GUIDE."

"He was only eighteen, but remains famous through-out this region." One of the race volunteers addresses the racers running in place to warm up. "He died saving a party of hikers who wandered off-trail, so we consider him a hero. Legend has it that his ghost continues to drift about these slopes, helping lost hikers."

The racers stop fidgeting and look at the speaker.

"But don't count on it!" the volunteer finishes with a chuckle, and we laugh nervously in response.

I pose beside the statue for a photo, stretching my arm in the same direction as the deceased guide. When I pat his concrete arm, it feels eerily warm, and his alert-looking eyes seem to follow me, even as I move away to line up with my team.

I lift my compass from its loop of cord attached to my wrist and check the map, which is made of a tough, waterproof paper. Then I mentally prepare, breathing in the moist rain forest smells and staring at bright pink flowers I've never seen before.

The start is staggered, each team signaled to begin according to when it arrived in Torotoro. When it's our turn, we plunge down the trail, the route firm in my mind. On either side of the trail, the undergrowth is densely woven, fragrant and full of strange, evil-looking, spiky plants.

Well ahead of Maria's team, we press on in silence. The rain brings nightfall sooner than we count on. David is complaining of a blister on his right foot. I'm feeling sore all over and am tired enough to wish I could drop down and sleep right in the middle of the muddy trail.

"Checkpoint No. 4," Dad says, pointing ahead, and we breathe a sigh of relief. Not just because it means we're on track, but because there's a tarp strung over a table where a volunteer is handing out bowls of hot soup. Better yet, they've put up a series of pup tents in a clearing for those who want to crawl in for some shut-eye. Nearby, a handful of racers is sitting around a campfire.

"We can eat and catch a few Zs here, right, Dad?" I ask as a volunteer stamps our passport.

Dad stretches, nods and checks his watch. "Okay, the usual three hours. But if you don't get up when I order you to, I'll send that ghost after you."

We line up for soup, then join the circle around the campfire: Mother, Dad and David on one side, Raul and me on the other. Members of an American team and an English team are conducting a lively debate as we perch ourselves on boulders.

"... fifty grand?"

"Don't believe it."

Someone does a low whistle.

"Hi." Dad smiles as he settles. "What's this about fifty grand? Prize money in an adventure race, I hope?" He chuckles.

"*Nah*. We're talking about that news item in Cochabamba about the baby broker who got caught," says a guy with a strong English accent. "Hugo Vargas. Sold hundreds of babies for years to rich couples for big money."

My dad seems alarmed as he and Mother exchange looks.

"So, how's the race going for you?" Dad addresses the group, trying to change the subject.

"Great. Anyway, what a scam! He pays doctors to help him find teenage girls who are pregnant, and then he offers the girls a home and free medical expenses till their babies arrive. Then if one tries to change her mind and keep her kid, he threatens her with a bill for everything he has spent on her! Shows her the contract she signed, and she doesn't know it would never, ever hold up in court. I know, 'cause I'm a lawyer. What a jerk!"

Mother has finished her soup in record time and stands up in a determined way. "I'll find a tent for us," she says and disappears into the dark before anyone can reply.

"Yeah," replies a tall American man, "but the real problem is all the couples who don't ask questions. Did that article really say they were paying fifty thousand dollars for a baby? Money like that in Bolivia—enough to turn anyone into a criminal."

"But if the girls don't want the babies, and the couples do, and someone is helping match them . . . ," my father says.

"Babies should never be for sale!" the English lawyer says, jumping up and all but dancing about as he points a finger at my dad. "There are licensed agencies for couples who want to adopt. Black-market ones are all about the money! The guys who run these operations aren't honest and don't keep proper records. So, unlike legal adoptions, the kid can't find his natural mother—or father—if he ever wants to. They don't give the couples the real story on the kid. And they don't check out the couple to see if they're even fit to be parents!"

"That's true," Raul inserts with vigor.

"But why would an adopted kid even want to find a mother who just gave him away, when he has a real family, the one that actually raised him?" David dares to ask.

The men stare at him. "How old are you, kid?" someone says with sarcasm.

Even in the firelight, I can see Dad is a bit rattled now. He gives us a pained look and rises, pulling David after him. "Raul and Andreo, you boys need to get some rest," he commands as the darkness swallows him, but we don't move.

"If they arrested this guy Vargas, why did they release him?" I ask.

"Well, it's tough to hold these guys 'cause neither the birth parents nor the adoptive parents are willing to come forward," the excitable guy from England says, noticing me for the first time. "So this scam artist has disappeared. Probably running around the country trying to scare up more girls he can hide away till it's time to sell their babies to the top bidder. Totally wrong, wrong, wrong!" The finger is now wagging at no one in particular.

I picture the beggar girls we saw on the steps of Vargas's former office building in Cochabamba. Raul and I only need to glance at each other to know we've heard enough.

David is pacing back and forth beside the soup operation with such concentration that he doesn't notice us steal by. As we creep closer to the tents, I hear Mother whispering something and Dad's low, comforting voice in reply.

"He doesn't know who arranged the adoption," he says. "And we didn't know it was illegal."

"We . . . should have," comes the firm reply.

Raul and I turn back. David is now sitting on the ground with his right boot and sock off, staring at a raw, puffy mess of blisters. I lower my backpack and pull out first-aid gear. "Let me dress that," I say, and he lets me without a word more between us.

CHAPTER EIGHT

The light rain has turned to a serious hammering by the time Dad shakes us awake. We pull on rain gear, switch on our headlamps and accept bowls of porridge from the tired-looking volunteers.

"Andreo, David would like to have a go at navigating this section," Dad addresses me.

"But I'm navigator, and I'm the one who has worked out the route!" I protest. Dad, of course, approved it earlier.

"We're proud you worked it out," Mother says, "and you remain chief navigator, but it's time David has a turn."

"Just a thought," Raul inserts hesitantly, "but jogging down a super-rocky mountain in the dark and rain and cold is where we need an experienced—"

"You know I can do it, so just hand it over," David says, grabbing the map from me.

Dad slips the compass from my wrist and places it around David's. As if I'd ever win where Mother and Dad have to choose between us.

"Whatever," I grumble. "Onward, fearless leader, and if we get lost, we'll all know whose fault it was."

Raul is correct about the challenge of this section. Climbing up to Checkpoint No. 4 before dark was tough enough. Doing a nighttime descent in a downpour is a horror show. Plus, three hours of sleep wasn't enough. Every one of us slips and flounders in the mud at some point. Soon we look like brown, mucky ghosts in our hooded rain gear. Five headlamps bob in single file. David leads; Raul and I take up the rear just out of earshot of the others.

"Wish we were still with Team Cochabamba," Raul grouses.

"And that would be for what reason?" I tease him.

He refuses to answer; he's obviously that smitten. So much for any designs I had on her.

"Well, we're faster than them. Had to happen sometime," I say.

There's silence as we work our way between giant boulders and down a treacherous, stepped, craggy ridge.

"Not much of a trail here," Raul says eventually.

"Or there is, and David has lost it," I say loud enough for the others to hear.

"Relax. He has been studying up. And he's a math whiz," Raul tries to reassure me.

"What's that got to do with it?" I grumble. "Anyone can count paces." I pause as a picture of the route I'd planned flashes into my mind. "Maybe my map memory is wrong, but I thought the trail dropped off the main ridge and picked up a narrow ridge to the east—back there in the boulder field. But hey, David's in charge."

"How long do you figure to the lake now?" Mother asks David, as everyone studiously ignores me.

"Six, seven hours."

"Good thing I've got The Man to keep me going," Raul says. He pulls earbuds out of his pocket and gets Bob Marley happening. Soon his headlamp is bobbing to the rhythm, and I'm left to my own thoughts as David leads us up and down—mostly down—this endless slope of mud, glistening boulders and dripping, leg-scratching bushes. There are no other teams within sight, but that's not unusual. I shiver and aim my light at my feet to minimize tripping and falling.

Bob Marley, or what I can hear of him, starts a new song, something about beauty. It gets me thinking about Maria and beauty queens.

"Doctor!" I suddenly shout.

Raul turns and takes out an earbud. "You okay?"

"Do you need a doctor?" Mother has rushed back to check on me.

"No, no," I say, embarrassed. "Just falling asleep on my feet, I think."

Mother hands me some chocolate-covered coffee beans for the caffeine, and Dad reminds us all to drink from our energy drinks at least every hour.

"Doctor," I whisper to Raul after everyone has resumed

their position. "If my mom really was a beauty queen, it means maybe my dad really is a doctor."

"Sure, you and me and the other five hundred and ninety-eight babies," he says in a low voice. "It was a sales pitch, stupid."

"Not for me," I say, and tell him about my Internet find—my birth mom's photo and the news she was from Torotoro. I dare not pull out the torn picture to show him here.

"Your mom's photo?" he whispers incredulously. "And we'll be in Torotoro in just twenty-four hours." Then he turns away and reinserts his earbuds, but not before I glimpse mixed emotions on his face. The fact that I'm making progress on finding my birth parents and he isn't is beginning to bum him out.

We've been going for more than an hour, the rain refusing to let up. I'm half-jogging, half-slithering, my mind on autopilot, when David approaches me, map in hand.

"Just want to double-check the route with you."

"You mean we're lost already."

He bristles. Dad comes to stand beside the two of us and gives me a warning look.

"We've come a couple of kilometers since that last junction, I figure," David says.

"Okay," I reply.

"And we were going to take this ridge bearing off to the east, right?" He's pointing to the map, which everyone has gathered around.

I think back to the terrain we've been traversing. I remember a short uphill section interrupting the relentless downhill of an undulating ridge—and wasn't there a broader plateau at one point, the one where I tripped and fell over a bush? (Where I really, really wanted to sleep rather than get up, as Dad made me do.) I study the map. I borrow back my compass and squint into the rainy blackness, which stubbornly obscures all features. I sigh.

"The ridge divides. See the plateau in between? You took us left at that junction, correct?" I ask.

"Yup, two kilometers ago," David answers.

"How do you figure two K?" I don't hide the impatience in my voice.

"Three hundred steps per kilometer. I've been counting."

He sounds proud. I want to kick him.

"Three hundred paces, David, not three hundred steps. A pace is two steps."

David frowns and hangs his head.

"So we wouldn't be at the ridge junction yet even if we were still on course! We must have taken this trail back here." I stab my finger at the map. "So much for the great math whiz!"

"Andreo!" Mother snaps. "Be respectful toward your brother. He's learning."

I point again at the map. "We've come a kilometer down the wrong ridge."

"What exactly are you trying to say, Andreo?" Dad asks in a warning tone.

"With all those boulder fields and the height we've lost, we're looking at a twenty-minute or longer scramble back up, then another ten to where we'd be if this idiot hadn't been put in charge," I say.

David balls his hand into a fist and lets fly. We tumble in the mud till Raul and Dad pull us apart. Then we get subjected to a Dad lecture about team cohesiveness, team spirit and brotherly love as Mother looks horrified.

For a split second, I contemplate sprinting away—leaving the entire team and racing to Torotoro, to where my birth mother was raised. I imagine her waiting for me with open arms in the door frame of a cute adobe house, an elaborate luncheon laid out on the table. In the backyard, my birth father will be swinging lazily in a hammock, and after lunch, they'll be eager to show me a collection of photo albums filled with pictures of other relatives eager to meet me.

"Andreo! Are you spacing out on us?" Raul nudges me.

I'm so tired, I have to put a lot of effort into pulling myself back to reality. "Best bet is to cut across the gully to our right," I finally say. "We'll lose height to begin with, but then it's only a short climb. I suggest we contour out to the southeast—maintaining altitude on this contour line—and pick up this other trail. Then we'll meet up with the one we would have been on in another ten kilometers."

Dad takes the map from my hands and studies it. His face looks haggard in the pooled light of our head-lamps. "Might be a rough descent. And there's a stream down there."

"I agree," I say, "and with all this rain, it could be interesting getting across it. But I still say it's better than retracing our steps."

David fidgets and stares at the ground.

"Andreo is right, team," Dad pronounces. "Just remember, we are a team and these things happen, especially with visibility so compromised." He sighs. "It'll set us back, but we're tough; we can handle it. And I take some responsibility for not keeping a closer eye on things."

"We'll make up some time risking the gully," I venture.

There's silence except for the pounding rain.

"My foot blisters are killing me," David finally dares to say. "Let's go for the gully. I'm sorry I went wrong, Andreo."

I swallow, and I want to say it's okay, that it was just a small error—we would, in fact, be right on track except for the math mistake—but the sight of Mother stroking David's elbow reassuringly seems to choke off my answer.

"Shall we take a vote?" Dad asks. Our headlamps reveal four for the shortcut, only Raul against.

"Okay, I'll lead," Dad says, and we're off, our heads bowed, our shoulders slumped, David limping.

"Why did you vote no?" I whisper to Raul.

"So Team Cochabamba can catch up with us," he replies with a smirk.

"They may yet, if this doesn't go well."

It doesn't go well. For one thing, the map is not as reliable as what we're used to. The gully is way steeper than indicated, and getting there cleans out my dwindling supply of energy. When we get to what must have been an insignificant stream earlier, we're faced with a torrent that makes my heart ram against my ribs.

"Form a chain," Dad commands. "Make sure you have a good foothold before you take the next step, and don't let go of anyone's hand."

He goes first. He's halfway across when he stumbles and just manages to right himself on a midstream boulder. The misstep is all it takes for Mother to go in. Without Dad's and David's lock-hold on her slim wrists, she'd have been swept all the way to who-knows-where by morning.

"I'm fine," she says bravely, though she's thoroughly soaked.

I watch David wince as his blistered foot searches for secure footing. Raul all but dances across after him, tugging me along. The water isn't icy like at home, but it's plenty cold. I'm utterly drained after the crossing.

Dad fishes dry clothes out of Mother's waterproof pack, despite her protests, then busies himself handing us all power bars while she changes.

As we slog on, I'm relieved Dad has taken over navigation duty. My mind is as numb as my body, and putting one foot in front of another is all I can manage. Still, I take satisfaction in noting that contouring out of the gully takes us to the lower trail and finally puts us back on course. How far now till the canoeing lake? With no more delays, I figure maybe we'll get there by mid-morning. I check my watch. It's 3:30 a.m.

Four, five and six o'clock pass in a blur before the first streaks of light appear on the skyline. Dad permits us a brief rest at some point, but without relief from the rain, it offers little respite. We haven't seen fellow racers now for hours. We're alone in Bolivian backcountry and on the brink of collapse. We resemble a pack of exhausted miners, headlamps bobbing in a downward march. I feel a steadying hand against my back, supporting me, pushing me forward.

"Thanks, Raul," I mumble sleepily.

I'm definitely sleepwalking, with only that hand to guide me, when I hear Mother shout, "Up there! Look!"

I blink and look up. Five bright stars are moving above us in the night, or maybe it's the lights of a UFO. Wait, no. They're headlamps. Adventure racers trudging southward, but they're a hundred feet immediately above us, like they're walking on air.

"Our shortcut worked. We'll soon be back on the main trail," says Dad with relief. "All we have to do is scramble up this last ridge."

I'm about to protest that I can't do it when I feel Raul pushing me gently, firmly again from behind. "Okay, okay," I say.

A hand reaches for mine as I near the top, where night is turning to dawn.

"About time," Raul says as he pulls me up.

I roll onto the muddy trail, breathing hard. I blink at Raul, then peer back over the ridge. I'm the last person up. There's no one below.

"You were in front of me this whole time?" I ask Raul.

"*Duh.*"

"Then who was behind me, helping me along?"

"No one."

"The ghost," David mocks me. "The guide who helps—"

"Those who get lost," I spit out at him.

CHAPTER NINE

I'm staring at a lineup of men in handcuffs, standing in various poses of defiance and feigned disinterest. I've been told all but one of them is a fake. Police Chief Ferreira taps me on the shoulder.

"Which one?" he asks.

"I don't know!" I answer for the third time, distressed at being pulled from the adventure race for this ridiculous exercise, and aware that my family and Raul are steaming with impatience outside the police station.

I look from one man to another again, from the one with bad teeth who glares at me in a sinister way, to one vaguely resembling the statue of the heroic mountain guide, to a man in a white coat with a stethoscope around his neck.

I point to the last man. "The doctor," I finally rule, "is my birth father."

"Excellent choice," says a deep voice behind me, and I turn to see the tall fat man in the black fedora nodding, chuckling and slapping his knee in delight.

———

Opening my eyes to a brilliant blue sky, I know I've been dreaming again. I'm lying full-length in the bottom of a cold aluminum canoe, still damp from the night's descent and eventual exit from Carrasco National Park. The unexpected cold makes me shiver. I have little memory of the final trek by daylight to this long brown lake surrounded by fields of wheat, broad beans and sweet potatoes. Vaguely, I recall Mother inspecting the canoes lined up on shore and muttering about how she was going to find us one without dents. As if a tiny dent or two was going to slow us down to the point we'd lose a place in this race. When I raise myself on my elbows, the boat rocks slightly.

"Easy, son," comes Dad's voice from the bow.

Mother, working the stern like she owns this lake— and like she hasn't been racing for almost thirty hours with only three hours' sleep—smiles brightly. "Good morning, Andreo."

"How long have I been asleep?" I ask, catching sight now of David and Raul in the canoe behind us, frantically trying to keep up so they can ride Mother and Dad's wake.

"Long enough to get the rest you needed," Mother says. "Want to give Dad a break now?"

"I don't need a break," Dad protests, but since no one is suggesting that Mother does—she's clearly happy in her favorite command post—Dad and I wriggle about till we've completed the swap. I've stroked less than five minutes when he starts snoring.

"You actually put David and Raul in the same canoe?" I tease Mother.

"They're way too busy trying to match our pace to argue," she replies lightly. "Three, two, one, swap sides."

Our paddles do the switch without losing a single stroke. We've been doing this together for as long as I can remember, and little is more peaceful, efficient and satisfying in life than paddling a canoe through water with my powerful mother.

"Land ahoy!" comes a shout from Raul.

We squint ahead and, sure enough, the mid-lake islet we've been waiting for is in sight.

"Checkpoint No. 5," David says in a tired but pleased voice. "We get a quick rest here, right? I so need a nap."

"Me too," says Raul, making me feel guilty that I've had one.

"Sure, one hour," Mother says in a low voice with a finger to her lips, pointing to Dad.

Springing out of the bow, I tie the canoe to shore, then beeline for the food table as Mother manages to step gingerly over Dad without waking him. Near the checkpoint, a row of snoozing bodies fills a tarp on the ground. I glance around and see other racers napping in their tied-up canoes. One team has pulled their canoe to shore and overturned it as a shelter for whoever is sleeping beneath it, his mud-caked shoes sticking out at an angle.

"Maria!" I hear David's and Raul's surprised voices greet our friend in unison.

"*Uh-oh*," I joke to Mother, who pretends she hasn't heard as she gets our team passport stamped.

Mother ends up chatting with some female competitors in the food line as David, Raul, Maria and I pile our plates with tostadas, corn cobs, potatoes, apples and a tasty local corn drink we're told is called *wilkaparu*. We plunk down on the ground for a picnic under the watchful eyes of Maria's dad and uncles. David and Raul vie for who can sit closest to Maria.

"Thought you guys were way ahead of us!" she exclaims. "How'd you get behind us?"

Raul explains how we got lost on the mountain, making sure she knows David was responsible.

"Hardly lost any time!" David counters, offering Maria his apple, which she refuses politely. "And look how we all but hydroplaned down the lake to catch you here. So let's paddle the rest of the way together, sound good?"

"*Ha*," she laughs lightly, "as if we could keep up with you."

"So, what's after the lake?" Raul asks her, even though he knows already.

"A short biking bit through some beautiful valleys, then some trekking through a gnarly set of canyons before we get to Torotoro. Torotoro, by the way, is Quechuan Indian for 'land of mud,' because in ancient times, it was supposedly a big lagoon. Anyway, that's where the caving part of this race is. I can hardly wait!"

"Where did you learn caving, Maria?" Raul asks, leaning in toward her. "In Cochabamba?"

"No way. We only moved to Cochabamba last year. I grew up in Torotoro. It has dozens of caves—more being discovered every day. Locals keep lots of them secret from visitors."

"Secret caves! Awesome," says Raul. "Maybe we could explore them on our day off."

She giggles, shoots a wary glance toward her uncles and then looks at Raul with sparkling eyes. "Why not?"

"Why not? Because it's our only rest day!" David snaps. "We're supposed to lay off activities to recover and get ready for the next leg!"

"David," comes Mother's shout. "Let me check your foot blisters."

"They're fine." David's cheeks turn bright red at the public announcement.

"Now, David," she insists, and he reluctantly rises and wanders off.

"Maria," I ask as soon as David is out of earshot, "I want to show you a photo and ask you a question. But I can't let my mother or David see me take it out of my pack."

"Okay," she says in a measured tone. "Raul, keep watch and warn us if anyone comes our way?"

"Ace spy, at your service."

We turn our backs and I pull out the photo.

"'VANESSA GUTIERREZ OF TOROTORO,'" she reads. "Where'd you get this? I've heard of her."

"You have?" I'm unable to hide my excitement at the news.

"It's not like my little village has had many beauty queens."

I pull out my birth certificate and point to my birth mother's name. Her eyes grow large. "Hey, Vanessa Gutierrez is your birth mother?"

"*Shhhh!*"

We peer at Raul, who's trying to blow a tune on some blades of grass between glances at Mother dressing David's foot.

"Know anything about her? Like where she might be now?"

Maria shakes her head. "No, but my grandmother lives in Torotoro, and she'd remember her."

My fingers clutch the photo tighter. "Can I talk to your grandma, Maria? On our day off tomorrow? To find out what I can?"

"Sure," she says amiably. She pulls paper and pencil from her backpack to scribble a name and address for me.

"Warning. Mother and brother on prowl," comes Raul's voice.

I shove the papers back into their plastic sheath and bury it deep in my pack. Maria stands and wanders a short distance away.

"David, Andreo and Raul, get some rest now, okay?" Mother points to the sleeping tarp and heads toward it. David stands awkwardly, shooting poison-dart eyes at Raul and me.

"Guys," Maria calls to the three of us, "come see this cool boulder over here." Her dad's and uncles' heads rise to watch us.

"You bet," Raul says, instantly by her side—but taking care not to stand too close, given the alert eyes of the bouncer-type uncles.

"Interesting," David says, joining us and stooping down to peer at a crevice in the boulder that resembles a dwarf's doorway.

"Who can squeeze through it?" Maria challenges us with a smile, dropping to her knees and arching her head back like a limbo dancer to pass through it gracefully.

Raul, master caver that he is, grins, contorts himself like a pretzel and eases through it as if he has done so a million times before.

I drop to all fours and squeeze through, nowhere near as smoothly as Raul.

David hesitates. "What if I get stuck?"

"You won't!" Maria encourages him. "Your chest will fit if you . . ." She trails off as he blushes deep red.

Right, she has noticed your chest size, bro. That totally means she's in love with you. NOT, you maniac.

David stands tall, puffs out his chest and moves toward the gap, making a show of visually measuring it.

"Attaway," Maria's father calls out. "Get 'im stuck solid. Then we'll beat 'em for sure."

David drops to his knees, tucks his elbows in, ducks his head and proceeds into the gap. Sure enough, he seems to get stuck. Maria flits to the opposite side to encourage him. Raul and I move around to watch from that angle too.

"I'm stuck—totally, totally stuck," he cries out, but there's something about his tone that seems wrong.

Maria, concern all over her face, offers him her hand. "You can do it, David. I know you can."

"Of course I can," he says, grinning, taking her hand and brushing his lips to her fingertips before leaping up to stand beside her. Maria backs away, startled and clearly distressed.

Oops. The bouncers may have had their view blocked, but Raul saw it.

"Hey!" He moves in and fists fly. My best friend and brother tumble to the ground, rolling this way and that.

"Asshole!"

"Creep!"

"Douche bag!"

They spin close to the bank. I hold my breath, then watch it happen as if in slow motion. *Splash!* Raul goes right into the water.

"*Ouch!*" David shouts, echoed by a clang as he lands half in and half out of our canoe.

One of David's knees goes into Dad's gut.

"*Argh!* What the hell?" Dad mumbles as he wakes and flails about so much that the canoe begins to rock.

Uh-oh. It's going to tip, I think as Raul swims to shore.

More splashing as the canoe upsets, spilling both David and Dad—not to mention our loose gear—into the water.

"*Ha-ha-ha!*" A crowd has gathered, laughing, pointing, clapping. Mother springs up, rubbing her eyes as if hoping she's dreaming. Then she and I are elbow-to-elbow, bent over to pull Dad and David out.

Dad and Raul turn the canoe upright, fetch the paddles and gear and bail out the canoe. We regroup and endure Mother and Dad's inevitable lecture: ". . . making a spectacle of our team . . . if you want to be grounded . . . serious family discussion about fighting . . . most important aspect of team racing is maintaining harmony."

"There go Maria and team," I whisper to Raul as we look out past the little island. He nods slowly, face glum. They're powering away, Maria huddled in the center, eyes cast our way like a subdued prisoner.

"We'll pass them, 'cause we're faster," he whispers back.

"And you know Mother and Dad will go way around them, even if it adds five minutes on to our race time," I reply evenly.

"Raul, you're in my canoe," Mother orders. "David, you're in Dad and Andreo's."

"Nice eye, David." Dad tries to lighten things up. "It's going to turn some very interesting colors before we reach Torotoro. Andreo and I will paddle first while you rest up."

"Catch us if you can," Raul says with a hint of satisfaction on his face.

"*Hmmph*," David mutters, laying himself full-length between Dad and me and pulling a wet T-shirt over his face.

As we work the paddles, I'm a little surprised at the effort it's taking to stay close to Mother and Raul. It seems my friend is paddling at a pace sure to impress his canoe-mate, maybe even take her mind off what he has done to her favorite son.

"The bike vans," I call out when the far end of the lake comes into sight.

"Yup, a quick transition, team. Ready?" Mother says.

As our canoes nose into the bank, we jump out, backpacks already on. We sprint to our waiting bikes as volunteers take over the boats.

I breathe in the smells of the verdant valley in which we've landed.

"Onward, team!" Dad calls as we lift our sore bottoms into bike saddles and wheel at high speed along a cobbled road hemmed by vegetable and fruit patches. Later, when the vans seem to magically appear again, it's time to dismount, hand our bikes over to the volunteers and continue on foot.

"Lunar landing," Raul comments as we take in a moonscape of reddish sandstone.

"Yeah, reminds me of the Badlands of South Dakota," Dad agrees.

"They could shoot Wild West movies here," David ruminates.

Indeed, I can easily imagine bandits on horses, waiting behind wind-sculpted rock formations.

Raul points to a craggy tower. "That's, like, a couple of stories high."

"It's cool," I say, but I'm impatient. I stick my head between Dad and David as they pore over the map. Though David has stopped asking to play navigator, I've noticed he lurks close when Dad and I have conversations and sometimes asks pertinent questions—intelligent ones, if I were forced to admit it. "We can make Torotoro by dark if we really push it, everyone," I say.

"You're right, Andreo," Mother says as Dad nods approvingly. Dad tucks the map into his pocket and we move faster.

Dry, steep creek beds snake torturously, breaking up any clear path like a maze, forcing us to retreat almost as often as we press ever southward.

"Torotoro," Dad mumbles an hour later in the near-dark as we spot a church steeple.

I stare, and somehow my exhaustion converts to elation. My birth mother's hometown.

"Tomorrow's a full day off," Mother says with a relief that we all feel. "Hot shower and bed tonight. Let's move it, team."

CHAPTER TEN

The bed is lumpy, the showers down the hall are out of hot water, and noise filters through the thin walls of our hotel room. But I've never slept so well or been so happy to have a bed as in Torotoro.

Sun has been streaming through the smudged windows for hours by the time I force my eyelids open. A day off: the very idea is awesome. And then I remember my mission.

I sit up in bed and stare across the room at David, snoring and spread-eagled in his boxers on his too-small hotel bed. His sheet is in a heap on the worn wooden floor; his eye is a ripe black-and-blue. Still sleeping soundly. Good. Raul's bed is empty, and it doesn't take me long to find his note: "Gone caving." *Why am I not surprised? No need to guess with whom.*

Pulling on clothes as fast as I can, I shoulder my pack and scurry past Mother and Dad's closed door. The stairs creak as I hurry down them. At the reception desk, I grab a map of the village and figure out directions to the address Maria has given me.

"I'll let my grandma know you're coming," Maria had said, and lucky for us, she'd managed to find a race volunteer willing to leave the phone message for her.

My feet tap out a rhythm on the rough pavement as I pass the windows of adobe houses. Inside, children in crisp school uniforms are eating their breakfasts. I smile at old women sweeping the sidewalks with straw brooms and men chewing coca leaves and joking in Quechuan while they wait in line for a truck to carry them to work. The smells of dust, fresh fruit and straw hats drift my way as vendors arrange fruit, fabric and other displays for sale.

The squeak of a piece of chalk makes me turn my head to see a pretty young woman writing the day's menu on a blackboard outside a café. Something Maria said about small, poor villages in Bolivia comes to mind: "They cannot live without smiling."

At the Internet café, after dashing in to determine that there's nothing from Detective Colque, I shoot him a few lines:

We're in Torotoro for two days: a day off, then the caving. I've learned that this is where my birth mother grew up, and I'm asking around. I may also try to see the doctor, in case he's my birth father. Any luck with information on

Raul's family or on where my birth mother has
ended up?

My fingers are crossed that the detective can help Raul,
not just me. Ten minutes later, I hesitate before an adobe
house with an old wooden door facing the main road.

It takes a lot of courage to lift my hand. *Knock, knock.*

I'm bowled back when a smiling, matronly woman in
a white blouse and long skirt throws the door wide open.
She raises her arms in greeting. "Andreo Gutierrez, yes?
I Maria's grandma, Olive de los Angeles. I so please to
meet you!"

My body freezes for a second. I've never been called
by the name on my birth certificate, and I also wasn't
expecting her to speak English. *Of course! Maria's father
is Australian. So the grandma has had time and a reason to
learn our language.*

"Come in, come in, come in!" she says, waving me
inside. "I make Arani bread, local specialty, and coca tea,
from our famosa coca leaves. A neighbor who knew your
mother more than me comes soon."

My race-stiffened legs shuffle in as I glance nervously
behind me for no good reason; it's not like my adoptive
parents would be hanging about at this end of town.

There are few rooms in the house, a large vegetable
garden out back. She ushers me into a central room that
seems to serve as dining and living room combined.
The scent of freshly cut irises rises from a vase in the

center of a table covered by a tablecloth featuring color-ful Andean folk designs.

"Is good you explore your Bolivian roots," Grandma de los Angeles says. "Maria phone message say so. And this race—is crazy sport my sons and Maria's father do. But gives you kids appetite, yes?" With this, she offers a plate of bread straight from the oven. My stomach rumbles.

"*Um*, thank you," I say, overwhelmed by her warmth and enthusiasm toward a total stranger. I sink my teeth into the soft bread and my taste buds dance all over the cheese flavor.

"Maria say tomorrow is caving part? Will be her favor-ite. She know all the caves around here very well. No can keep her nose out of them. Why this interest in dark, dangerous places?"

She pours us tea, seats herself on a faded sofa and draws a small white kitten into her lap. It eyes me lazily as it stretches and flicks its tail back and forth.

"Never knew well your mother. Knew her parents, God rest their souls. Little Vanessa was quiet girl, always did what told. She pretty. Win beauty contest once, like my Maria. Her parents so proud."

"Proud," I repeat dumbly, not knowing what else to say.

"And I remember when they throw her out of their home. We could all guess why. Oh yes, so sad. They hand her sack with her clothes. Lock door, ignore her crying. The poor dear. She was only seventeen." The cat settles into a small, furry ball and purrs under the grand-mother's stroking.

"Did she, does she . . . have sisters or brothers here?" I ask.

"Oh, she have two older sisters, but even if still lived here, they slam their doors so hard in your face that your nose go flat. Their own marriage chances were hurt by her . . . scandal. They move away."

"I see. And my birth father?"

"No idea, *cariño*. Only your mother knows that."

"*Um*, are there any doctors in Torotoro?"

"Oh dear, you are sick?"

"No, no, but my brother has a bad blister that maybe needs looking at," I lie.

"*Ah*. Well, is just one doctor here—has been in town twenty years. Nice man. Clinic is beside his house." She gives me directions.

I'm racking my brain for more questions when there's a loud knock.

"*Ah*, is Ardillita, my neighbor."

"Ardillita?" I echo nervously, sitting up straight.

"Hello, Mrs. de los Angeles. We're here!" comes a high, lighthearted voice in Spanish from the doorway. "Juan Pedro is off work so he has come with me, along with our three youngest—couldn't leave them home. I knew you wouldn't mind."

She's stout and lively looking, around thirty, wearing a crisp white blouse and gathered skirt. She has two waist-length black braids whose ends are joined in a tiny beaded sack. She's also wearing a colorful *aguayo*—a bright, striped cloth flung across her shoulder and back holding a wide-eyed baby in a woolen cap not unlike my baby one.

"Mama?"

Looking for the voice, I see a toddler boy clinging to her legs.

Behind her is a man her age, short but strongly built, with black hair, a mustache and teeth slightly green, presumably from chewing coca leaves. He wears black sandals, a white T-shirt, a vest and ripped, faded jeans held up by a colorful belt. One hand rests on the thick hair of a boy around five.

"*Hola*," I say, my voice soft and shaky.

The visitors stare shyly at me—I feel like it's some kind of freak show—except Ardillita, who rushes up with a broad smile and pumps my hand. "Andreo Gutierrez, I am Ardillita Espada and this is my husband, Juan Pedro, and three of our six. The older ones are at school, of course." She speaks slowly and clearly so I can understand her Spanish. Grandma de los Angeles translates when I don't.

"*Hola! Encantado!*" The husband shakes my hand, then retreats to the sofa, where his wife soon joins him.

"Papa!" cries the older boy. As Juan Pedro lifts him into his lap, the toddler careens across the floor to press his face into his dad's vest.

I wink at the kids, and Juan Pedro's humming fills the room.

I watch Grandma de los Angeles trundle out of the room with empty dishes, emerging moments later with a tray laden with more bread and tea.

"Mrs. de los Angeles asked me to come over to tell you what I know about your mother," Ardillita says. "I'm two years younger than her. I was fifteen when my parents sent me to Cochabamba for the same reason Vanessa's parents sent her."

She waits for that to sink in. "The big difference between us is that my parents allowed me to come back to Torotoro. They were brave that way."

I nod.

"Vanessa was nice to me while we were there, even though we barely knew each other before that."

My throat goes dry. *What does she mean by "there," exactly?*

"Hugo Vargas arranged it all." Her eyes narrow, and bitterness infuses her voice. "The scruffy, overcrowded house in Cochabamba. The housemother who cooked and washed for us—and made sure we never left the house without her. The nurses and doctor who checked us. And all the paperwork that allowed people in North America to steal our babies."

My head jerks up at the word "steal." The hint of a smile appears on her face, as if she's pleased that it has gotten my attention. She shifts the baby in her lap and reaches out to hold hands with her husband.

"After Vanessa had you," Ardillita continues, "she stayed on to help the housemother. Nowhere else to go but the streets, I suppose. She was good to me."

Was she devastated at having lost me? I want to know. *Did she fight it? Has she searched for me since? Is she still alive?*

"A month before I had my baby, I panicked. I decided I didn't want it sold. I told Mr. Vargas I wanted to keep it, even if I had to beg on the streets with it in my arms. He produced all kinds of forms I'd signed. Said I had no choice. I confided to Vanessa that I was going to run away. She seemed sympathetic, but couldn't help me. The housemother watched us all very closely. I wasn't even allowed out of the house the last while. When it was time for the baby to arrive, things didn't go well. They had to give me some drugs to help me. When I woke up, my newborn girl—the housemother and Vanessa told me it was a girl—was gone. Stolen."

Ardillita's face crumples. She covers it as she sobs for a moment. Her husband strokes her back and whispers, "It's okay, it's okay."

After a moment, she raises her chin. "I told Hugo Vargas I would never, ever stop trying to find my child. He laughed."

"And did you find her?" I ask. This only produces more sobs. The three children are wide-eyed to see their mother's face buried in their father's neck.

"When Juan Pedro and I eventually married," she

finally continues, "we swore we'd save until we could afford a lawyer to find our daughter."

I glance at Juan Pedro. "Yes, *our* daughter," he says in a quiet voice.

"We eventually did hire someone, and he tried. Vargas must not have liked that, because we started getting anonymous threatening notes and suspicious people following us—even here, hours from Cochabamba. In the end, the guy we hired could do nothing. Vargas was too clever. There was no paper trail to follow. And no one could lay a hand on Vargas. Until now."

"*Huh?*"

"He has been arrested. Released, yes, but the police will get him in the end. Soon, I hope. We'll testify. He knows it. And they'll find others. That's why he's hiding, so they say."

Silence weighs on us for several moments. The two older children have crawled down from Juan Pedro's lap to play with the kitten. The clink of dishes being washed sounds from the kitchen.

"Do you know who my birth father is?" I ask. It comes out in a weak croak.

Ardillita shakes her head sadly.

"And my mom. What happened to her?" My voice trembles.

"I saw her once after I returned from Cochabamba. A year or two later. She was in Torotoro just for the day; she stopped to see me. She had a wedding ring on. She told me she was happy; she looked happy. She wouldn't tell me who she married or where she was going. She'd heard that Juan Pedro and I were engaged. She just wanted to wish me well. She also urged me to forget the baby I lost and to look forward rather than back."

Like she did? "So there's nothing more I can do to try and find her?"

Ardillita rises and walks over to where I'm sitting. With no warning, she leans down and hugs me, hard. I want to struggle loose, but somehow I know she needs this—to feel some kind of connection with one of Hugo Vargas's stolen children. *Do not pretend she's Vanessa*, I tell myself.

Tears spill down her cheeks again as she releases me. "The police will get him. Maybe then you'll learn something," she says. "Maybe I will too. Remember, no mother can forget or stop loving, even if she's forced to hide the pain deep in her heart."

CHAPTER ELEVEN

Once again, my shoes make their way over the cobblestones as Ardillita and Juan Pedro walk me to the town square.

"*Dinosaurio!*" exclaims the oldest boy. As we stare at a giant fiberglass dinosaur, I wrap my arms around his little waist and lift him high to let him touch its teeth. We're both laughing as he squirms in mock fright.

"*Hasta la vista,*" Ardillita says as she bear-hugs me good-bye. Juan Pedro slaps my back like we're old friends, and then I head to the Internet café.

```
Well done, Andreo.
   Yes, your mother was born and raised in
Torotoro, and I am delighted you have managed
to come up with contacts and information to
further our search. Congratulations also on
finishing most of the race already. I know you
are biking back toward Cochabamba after the
```

caving tomorrow, so if you can just e-mail me
the info you've gathered, I'll pursue it and
hopefully have something new for you by the
time you get back here. Maybe I should hire
you, given your sleuthing talents!

Together, we'll find Vanessa, I hope before
you fly home. Also please let me know if you
change your mind about persuading your parents
to sign a statement about their dealings with
Hugo Vargas, okay?

Detective Colque

My fingers fly over the keyboard as I explain about
Maria, her grandmother, Ardillita and Juan Pedro and
all they've relayed to me. I tell him I'll sneak away from
my parents at the race's finish to visit him the minute
I can. I end the message, My parents must not be
involved in this at all!

I've just pushed SEND when hands land heavily on
my shoulders.

"Raul! You scared me!" I twirl around to see my
friend displaying the world's largest grin. He plops down,
face glowing, to tell me all about his caving adventures
with Maria.

"This place is utterly awesome, *mon*. We did an explor-
atory on a cave that reminded me of that bear cave back
home. And she showed me a couple of other caves, including one place so huge it's like a cathedral with big arched

ceilings. People even pay to get married there. Everything today was just totally, unbelievably awesome!"

"Totally, unbelievably awesome," I mock him. "And Maria is . . ."

". . . totally, unbelievably awesome too, Andreo." He feigns pulling a knife out of his heart. "Don't want this race to end, *mon*."

I roll my eyes, but I'm happy for him. I tell my story rapid-fire, all the while keeping an eye on the door. "So, Raul, hurry up and check your e-mail, and let's get back to the hotel before Mother and Dad send out a search party. I never even left a note."

He opens up his e-mail and I watch his face go from over-the-top happy to pale.

"What's up?"

"Dad got arrested for drunk driving."

"I'm sorry," I say, like I have a ton of times before.

"And this time," he says, lowering his face to cup it in his hands, "he's going to jail."

Uh-oh. That's new. "I'm sorry." I struggle for something else to say.

He turns his head so I can't see his face. "And Mom's leaving him. Divorcing him."

I jump as his fist comes down hard beside the computer. "My family sucks. Totally sucks. Why bother going home?"

We sit in stunned silence. I reach out to touch his shoulder, but he slashes my hand away.

"We're not fighting, are we?" asks a sarcastic voice. "Where the hell have you two deserters been all day, anyway?"

David, just who we need.

"David, we're about to head back to the hotel. Can you leave us alone till then?" I ask. "Where are Mother and Dad?"

He moves closer, shifts off his blistered foot, then stands with his hands on his hips, studying Raul before turning back to me.

"Tell you what, brother dearest. I'll tell you where they are if you tell me why Mom is so upset. Something about seeing you with people you seem to know in the dinosaur square?"

I freeze and look at Raul; he's slumped in his chair, arms around himself. *Distraction time.* "David," I say, "it smells like your foot is infected. When was the last time anyone treated it?"

"My foot is fine," he declares, but his eyes shift to it.

"Not," I say in my most concerned voice. "You know what Dad says about my sense of smell. Your sores are starting to get infected. I know where the doctor is in this town. How about I show you? Raul, we'll see you back at the hotel."

Raul doesn't respond as I put an arm around David's shoulder and steer him out of the café.

"It's just blisters," my startled brother says.

"Infected blisters during an adventure race can be a

disaster. You know that." We're headed up cobbled streets to where Maria's grandmother told me the doctor's clinic is located.

Walking together with arms around each other's shoulders feels weird. Like when we were six and performing in a three-legged race: Mother's "twins." But even back then, I don't remember laughing and tumbling around together in fun, like normal brothers. I was too busy competing for Mother's love.

"What's up with Raul?" David interrupts my thoughts.

I tell him Raul's news from home. He goes quiet for a moment. "Sucks to be Raul," he finally says, but I detect no sarcasm. He really means it. "You know, I prefer the four-person adventure races," he says, changing the subject as we slow down on a steep uphill.

"You mean, when Raul's not with us."

"Yeah. I mean, when it's just family, you and I can hang out. When Raul's around, you guys are such a unit. To be honest, I get a little jealous. And it forces me to be with Mom and Dad all the time."

Hang out? Jealous? Since when are he and Mother and Dad not their own permanent, impenetrable unit? His face reddens at my lack of response. "You really think I need to go to the doctor about this foot?"

"I think it needs a professional opinion, maybe some prescription ointment," I lie.

"Thanks, Andreo," he says, stopping and looking at me all serious-like. I feel a stab of guilt. We've reached the clinic. I'm losing my nerve for going inside. *A beauty queen and a married doctor. And this is the only doctor in town, been here twenty years.*

"I mean," David is saying, his face reddening further, "I wasn't sure anyone really cared. Mom was dressing it, but she and Dad were both saying that the trekking part's over and it won't mess much with caving and biking, so I should tough it out."

"Sounds like Mother and Dad," I say. "Ignore it, suck it up, carry on like it's not there." *Especially if it involves acknowledging birth parents or adoption.*

David spins around and puts his arm back on my shoulder. "I can't believe you said that. It's so true. Andreo, can I tell you a secret?"

There's a temptation to brush his arm off and run. I'm not sure which is worse, my hand on a door I'm scared to open, or David's arm on me. But I say, "Go for it," a new helping of guilt weighing on me.

"When this race is over, I'm going to stop adventure racing. I don't want to compete anymore."

"No?" Chickening out, I back away from the clinic door. At the same time, I catch a glimpse of the doctor's small house near its rear door, like Maria's grandma said.

"I don't even want to do track at school. I just want to concentrate on grades. But Dad's going to freak. Maybe . . . maybe you can back me up? Argue for me? I didn't think I'd have the nerve to ask you, but, but . . . You do get how they are. I'm just not athletic like you. To be honest, Andreo, I've always been jealous . . ."

"Let's go in and deal with your foot," I say brusquely.

His face falls. My insides twist with shame, but my nerves are totally jangled by the possibility of meeting my birth father. And David—or some weird version of him—is seriously increasing my anxiety level.

"Okay," David says. "We'll talk about it some other time. But while I have you alone, I have to ask you something else."

"What?" Hopefully I don't sound impatient.

"Are you and Raul up to something? I mean, the way you guys whisper and sneak off and keep checking the Internet. And the way you got Mom upset about something this afternoon. Are you in trouble?"

"We're not up to anything that concerns you." It comes out through gritted teeth.

He nods slowly but doesn't look convinced. "And it's nothing that will hurt Mom or Dad?"

"Nothing that should hurt Mother or Dad." *I'm making sure they won't find out, and anyway they have no right to feel hurt by our gathering information they should have given me ages ago!*

Pushing the door open, I step into the clinic, David on my heels. He hangs back, maybe because my Spanish is better.

"Can I help you?" asks a tall, broad receptionist with an unfriendly face. The room is small and plain, with stiff curtains on the windows and green walls. A lineup of metal chairs is occupied by patients who pretend not to stare at me.

I feel a drop of sweat trickle down my back. "*Um*, my brother here needs to see a doctor about some blisters that may be infected." At least, that's what I hope my limited Spanish has said.

"Dr. A is on lunch break."

"You mean, in his house behind the clinic?" I can't believe I say that.

She stiffens. "Does Dr. A know you? What's your name?"

I lean in so close that she pulls back, but I have to make sure that David, who has taken a seat near the door, doesn't hear.

"I'm Andreo Gutierrez. Son of Vanessa Gutierrez. I'm sixteen."

She stares at me coldly. The name obviously means nothing to her, and for a moment, I think she's going to throw us out. Then she turns on her heel and goes out the back door. The bell on it jingles as she disappears.

I take a deep, steadying breath and glance behind me. David is calmly turning the pages of a magazine. I look down to see my own hands shaking. I count slowly to ten. The jingle sounds again and I look up. The receptionist enters, then I'm staring at Dr. A, who is staring back at me. He's black. Behind the desk, I notice a photo calendar of Rwanda.

"Dr. Zacharie Akumuntu," he says, all businesslike. "You have some kind of emergency?"

Seeing me struggling for words, David leaps up, shakes hands with the doctor and says. "*Es, um, necesario*—to have a—*tener una, um, cita*? An appointment?" Before I can pull myself together, the door clicks as the two disappear into an examination room.

Not my birth father is echoing through my head as I lower myself into a waiting room chair. I'm so humiliated that I don't notice when a woman clutching a baby enters the clinic and slides into the seat beside me.

"Andreo," Ardillita is whispering, even though no one else in the room but the icy receptionist pays attention. "Your mother is in Torotoro. Andreo? Are you okay? I saw Vanessa an hour ago."

I sit bolt upright and look at her.

"Mrs. de los Angeles said she'd given you the clinic's address, so I hoped I'd find you here. I saw Vanessa in the marketplace. She was buying food. I recognized her even though she had a scarf pulled partway around her face. But when I headed over to say hi, she disappeared. I don't know if she actually saw me."

I glance at the receptionist, now busy taking a phone call. I look at the examination room door, still closed.

"Ardillita," I say with urgency, "do you have a cell phone on you?"

She hands it to me with a smile; I rush outside and phone Detective Colque.

"You're certain?" he says, his voice rising with excitement. "This Ardillita is sure it was her?"

"She's sure."

"Okay, Andreo. This is our big break. Tell me, what time do you leave the hotel for the caving event tomorrow? Nine o'clock? Good. Do you still want to meet your birth mother, son?"

I choke up. "Yes."

"Of course you do. So, go back to your hotel. Check with the receptionist there for a message from me before you go to bed. I'm on my way to Torotoro. I will track her down, and I will set up an early-morning meeting that won't interfere with your race."

"My parents can't know anything about this."

"Don't worry," he says and clicks off.

I step back into the clinic, glance at the receptionist and the closed examination-room door and whisper to Ardillita, "I'm meeting her tomorrow."

Her eyes light up. She gives me a quick hug and takes back her phone. "E-mail me about it," she begs, her eyes glistening. As she slips out the door, I look up to see David frozen in front of me. There's no sign of Dr. A.

"Just a blister," he says slowly, eyes boring into me. "Who was that?"

"Friend of Maria's."

"Sure," he says coldly.

Okay, so we're back to being brenemies.

CHAPTER TWELVE

Running joyously over the uneven cobblestones, running like I'm flying, running to her open arms.

"Mom!" I mumble into her peasant blouse as she embraces me.

"Andreo!" she replies, the warmth of her voice enveloping and lifting me like the pinkish dawn of the day.

"Ask me anything; tell me all about you," she says as we step back, still holding hands, looking into one another's faces. "But before you start, I have a question: Will you come live with your birth father and me?"

The cobblestones under my feet tremble, or is it my knees? I look down to see the stones shake more violently, then push upward and shatter. *This is a dream, right?*

I'm running over the heaving cobblestones. My birth mother is several steps ahead of me, her sandaled feet moving like they know every inch of the way. The distance between us is growing. Is she trying to run away?

"Mom!" I cry. "I have so many questions for you!"

She turns just long enough for me to see the distress in her dark eyes. "I got rid of you once!" she shouts. "Why have you come back?" And then she's gone.

I'm dreaming. My dreams don't mean anything.

The ground stops quaking, a thin fog descends and she halts. I stand there, uncertain. I yearn for an embrace, and my heartbeat rises as she opens her arms, but this time she walks right past me, eyes on someone behind me. I turn and watch her clasp Raul's hands.

"Raul?" I demand. "What are you doing here?"

But he acts like I'm not there. He allows my birth mother to guide him to a bar that materializes as the fog rolls away. I follow them in. The stench of stale beer assaults my nostrils; shrieks, laughter and music half-deafen me.

"*Whoo-hoo*! It's Vanessa!" a couple shouts to my birth mother, raising their hands and staggering toward her from the bar.

"Raul," my birth mother murmurs, "meet your birth parents."

The couple laughs and clinks their glasses together, sending liquid sloshing to the sticky floor. They giggle as they eye Raul. "Who'd you say this is?" they slur.

"It's okay," I promise Raul as his face falls. "We're just dreaming."

I wake in a sweat minutes before my watch alarm is due to beep and shake the dreams from my head. It's 6:00 a.m.

Dressing quickly in running gear, I scribble a note to leave on my bed: "Gone for a run."

Then I steal out, hoping that the click of the door doesn't wake Raul, who knows what I'm up to, or David, who has hardly said a word to me since our clinic visit. Try as I might to banish thoughts about dinner last night, it all comes back in a rush:

"Okay, Team Family Dynamics, time to discuss caving strategy," Dad says after we order our food.

From where she and Raul are huddled and speaking softly at the end of the table, Mother raises her head. "Not now, honey. Give Raul and me a moment, please."

Raul, pale-faced and head hung low, the cola he'd ordered untouched, doesn't look like he's even listening to Mother's attempts to comfort him.

So David filled Mother and Dad in on Raul's family problems, *I reflect.* Busybody.

"Mother?" I say, trying to pass her the basket of bread.

Her hand rises to push it away gently; as her distant eyes meet mine, I feel it's not the bread that she's rejecting. Is it because she saw me at the dinosaur square?

"So right from the start, we need to establish the order of our lineup, before any part of the cave narrows," Dad says. "David, are you even listening? You keep staring at the doorway like you're expecting the queen."

"More like Maria and her family," I say.

"Shut up, Andreo," David volleys back, his face reddening.

"Give it up, more like," I reply.

"Boys! Can you please give me your attention! The caving, remember? And Pearl, Raul, enough already with the secret conversation down there. Especially you, Raul. You're our caving leader. . . ."

"Andreo!" Detective Colque greets me at the hotel desk, pulling me back to the present.

Whew, he's here just as he promised he'd be, even if he does smell of too much cologne.

I shake his hand and we head across town, me sweating like I really am on a training run.

"Thanks for driving all the way from Cochabamba last night," I say.

"No thanks needed, Andreo. This is the best part of my job."

The first orange-pink rays of light are shimmering on the horizon as we near the doctor's clinic.

"How'd you find her?" I ask, hoping conversation will steady my nerves.

"I have contacts all over, as any good detective should," he replies with a wink. "Dr. A is one of them."

Through the drawn curtains of the clinic, a light glows weakly. The sign on the door reads CLOSED in Spanish. Detective Colque's hand is on the small of my back, pressing me forward gently. "It's unlocked. She's waiting inside. She's fluent in English, by the way. Works as a secretary for an international firm that requires it. I'll be here when you're finished." Before I can protest, he melts away into the dawn.

My sweaty palm barely manages to twist the doorknob. I gaze at the far side of the room, where a slim woman is knitting furiously under a pool of light from a floor lamp. The needles freeze. She lifts her face.

"Andreo?" says a voice that sounds much younger than her years. She sets her knitting aside and rises, her steps hesitant, her forehead moist.

She looks barely older than the beauty queen printout I have. Dark braids, almond eyes, high cheekbones and a long, graceful neck. She's wearing a simple blouse and gathered skirt, the kind all the indigenous women around here seem to wear, but the pink sweater is fancy and she has heels on. Tiny diamond earrings sparkle in the limited light. I move closer. There's something between longing and fear in her eyes. In all my dreams, I never imagined I would have to be the one to put her at ease.

"Yes, I'm Andreo," I say, my chest so tight I'm amazed the words squeeze out. I lift my trembling hands to hers. She smiles, almost like she's forcing it, and then she suddenly throws herself forward and wraps her arms around me, pulling me in so tight that I'm half-smothered by the soft wool of her sweater—the same softness as the wool of my baby cap.

"I've waited for this a very long time," she mouths into my shoulder, which is as far as her head reaches. I bury my face in her silken hair as I have a thousand times before, but this time it's no dream. She smells of rose perfume.

"You really are Van—"

"Call me Mom," she says in a choked little voice. She grips my hands and separates us to gaze at me. Her long lashes blink rapidly. "How did you find me, Andreo?"

"My adoptive parents finally showed me my birth certificate—sort of. Plus I saw the Internet article about Hugo Vargas"—I detect her involuntary wince as I mention his name—"and help from Ardillita and Detective Colque, of course."

"Detective Colque is a good man," she says, producing a handkerchief to dab at the corners of her eyes. Her fingernails are long and painted a pink that matches her sweater. "If only Ardillita could find her daughter like I've found you."

Silence weighs on us for a moment or two. She reseats herself and motions me to sit beside her.

"You have my nose," she says with a light, nervous laugh. My hands move to my nose and we both laugh. "Tell me about yourself, Andreo. Everything!" She pulls her knitting into her lap and gives me an expectant smile. I watch her needles begin to click again.

I launch into a disconnected speech about how the adventure race brought me to Bolivia. I tell her of my love for sports and describe our house in Canada and the snow-covered mountains and great caves in my community. I tell her about my school and my friend Raul, and I mention that I have one brother. "Not adopted," I add a little tensely. I tell her what my mother and father do for a living but don't elaborate.

She nods and sniffs as if trying not to cry. Her needles are going so fast, they're a blur. "I hoped you would go to a good family and have a good life, Andreo. That is all I ever dared hope for you. You do understand I had to give you up, don't you? I had nothing, absolutely nothing. It was the most painful thing I ever did, but I did it for you."

She raises a hand to wipe at her eyes. My own chest has gone hollow and my eyes are stinging. I notice a wedding ring on her finger. At length, she follows my eyes. "I'm sure you have questions for me, Andreo. I'll answer those that I can, okay?"

I'm trying to form all the questions I've put to her in dreams for years, but my throat isn't cooperating. "You're a secretary," I finally say.

"Yes."

I look again at her ring but can't push the question out.

"Yes, I'm married," she says with a smile. "Very happily." Her face glows for the first time, and I know she means it. "Not to your father." She watches my own face fall.

"I've never told anyone who your father was. No one. But you deserve to know. It was Marcelo Quispe, the trail guide they honor over in Villa Tunari. He was a caving guide here in Torotoro, just briefly, before he went there." She actually blushes, and it makes her even more beautiful than she is already. "He died just before you were born."

She hangs her head as if the memory remains heavy.

I nod. "Thank you for telling me." I try to picture the young man's statue. I recall getting my photo taken next to it. I wonder if it was my birth father's ghost who helped me that rainy night. Or just delusions from exhaustion.

"Except for your nose, you look a lot like him. And you're strong and athletic like him. He was an exceptional guide, anyone will tell you. He was at home in the outdoors in any weather, good with people and a born navigator."

My chest seizes up; my eyes go watery. With difficulty, I get control of myself. "Do you have other children?"

She shakes her head firmly no. "I've not been blessed that way. Which may be why I've thought of you so often over the years."

"Do you know who my friend Raul's birth parents are?" I ask. "His birth certificate gives his name as Raul Apaza."

She stiffens. Her face goes taut. The needles hang in the air. I've obviously crossed some kind of line; I could kick myself for it.

"No, Andreo," she finally says. "I'm sorry." Her eyes won't meet mine. She must know something, but I dare not push it.

A soft rap on the door makes us both jump. Detective Colque pushes his head in. "Andreo, you're not keeping track of time. We don't want your adoptive parents searching for you, do we? And patients will be lining up for the clinic anytime now." He steps back outside.

I check my watch and panic. I look at my mother— my real mother—who has resumed knitting like no one has disturbed us. Lifting my backpack into my lap, I rummage through it to produce my baby cap.

She stares at it, drops her knitting and hugs me tightly again. Her face is buried in my chest. Somehow, that emboldens me. "Mom, where do you live? Why are you in Torotoro? What's your last name? What does your husband do? Can we write to each other? Do you want to see me again?" I can't believe I've gone from having difficulty asking a question to having them spill one over another.

She doesn't move. I want to see her face, I need to see her face, but I'm unwilling to break our embrace.

Detective Colque enters and stands there, glancing worriedly from us to the front door.

She rises slowly, smoothes her hair, pushes her knitting into a bag. She picks up my baby cap, fondles it for a moment, then returns it to me. She takes my hands in hers. The almond eyes gaze a bit distantly at me; I drink in her rose scent and wait.

"You can always contact me through Detective Colque," she says. "I'm so glad you found a loving home,

Andreo. Embrace it. It's something I never had, once I was pregnant with you."

I open my mouth to reply, gripping her hands tighter, but the dainty fingers with their pink painted nails slip out easily. She turns and disappears out the back door.

"Andreo," Detective Colque is saying, "I'll walk you back to the hotel. How did it go, on a scale of one to ten?"

"Ten," I mutter. *Except that I didn't want it to end.*

"That's good," he says soothingly. "Believe me, these reunions don't always go as people hope. You'll return to Canada satisfied, then."

Satisfied. Satisfied. The word doesn't sit right. But how could anyone who hasn't spent a lifetime wondering about their birth parents ever find the right words to say at a time like this?

CHAPTER THIRTEEN

David's waiting for me in our hotel room, suspicion written all over his face.

"Where's Raul?" I ask before he can say anything.

He waves a note in my face. "Also out for a run. Seems to be the thing to do this morning, even though we should be saving our energy for caving. And yet, curiously, you two were not running together?"

I shrug as casually as I can. "I woke up before him. Anyway, it's good to get the blood flowing before we head to the caves."

"Well, I hope you're going to shower before I have to crawl around tight spaces with you." He pinches his nose shut for effect.

"You bet." After grabbing my towel and some clothes, I head down the hall. In the shower, I lather up and luxuriate in the steamy hot water, trying to come down from the high of finally meeting my birth mother and learning the identity of my birth father.

Only as I step out of the shower do I realize I've left my backpack in my room. Wearing nothing but a towel, I sprint down the hall, dodging a couple of female hotel guests who cover their mouths and giggle.

The door swings open to reveal David rifling through my pack, the birth documents and baby cap set aside on his bed. Raul enters the room just as I perform a flying leap to grab the papers.

David offers no resistance, just stands and directs an evil smile at Raul and me.

"You have no right!" I shout.

"Oh, but I do," he replies in an ominous tone as he points at me. "Because you've been lying and sneaking around and compromising our team effort for this other thing—this, this chase after your birth parents, is that it? Is that who knitted this stupid little hat?" He perches it on his hair, then pulls hard on it to try and stretch it over his head. I attempt a tackle, but he raises his knee with just the right timing to slam it into my groin.

I land on the floor writhing in my wet towel. "You bastard," I cry.

Raul has retreated silently to his own bed to watch.

"Bastard is a better term for *you*, Andreo," David replies, drawing himself up like he's a judge holding some kind of court. "Father unknown. Mother a teen slut who got rid of you the first chance she could. You get lucky and land in a nice home, and what do you do to show your appreciation? You grow up all resentful. You treat me like I'm some kind of lesser being all our lives. And then you accept an all-expenses-paid trip to the land of your birth, pretending you want to race as part of that family. When you're really planning to investigate your roots and probably take off at the first opportunity. Have I got that right?"

"Don't tempt me," I say hoarsely, still doubled up with pain. I want nothing more than to sink my fist into his face.

"Not only do you have a whore for a mother, but she goes to a black-market criminal to sell her baby for the highest price. Hugo Vargas signed your Order of Adoption, I see. He's the one the police arrested, correct?"

"You don't know anything!" I shout.

"Or maybe I do," he says, tugging on a tassel of my baby cap, then flicking it back and forth in front of his face. "Well, brother dearest, why don't you just run away and have a perfect life here in Bolivia? It's where you belong. Mom, Dad and I can get along just fine without you. We're *real* family. A bloodline, get it?"

I start to leap up, my fist primed, but Raul moves faster. He sits on my chest, holding me down on the bare floorboards, his hands locking both my wrists until I stop struggling.

"You're a first-class jerk, David," I call out from where I'm trapped. "Selfish as Mother and Dad, only ever thinking about yourselves and racing. Pretending I'm not adopted. Forbidding a conversation about it. Sweeping it all under the rug because Mother can't handle the fact I have another mother, a real mother." I let my voice rise to falsetto for the full sarcastic effect.

"For your information," I continue, "I *have* met my birth mother, just this morning, and she *is* perfect. She never got a penny for me. And my real father isn't unknown. He was a highly respected guide around here. He died before I was born. I look like him. And it wasn't my mother's choice to give me away," I lie as a finishing flourish.

Raul is frowning, and still crushing my chest where he's sitting astride me. But there's no stopping me now. "Raul and I can wander around Bolivia without anyone thinking we're foreign. You know how that feels? After being stared at and questioned and made fun of our entire lives? No, you have no idea. Because you've spent your whole cushy life being Mother and Dad's favorite and fitting right in. Being a wimpy spoiled brat who can't even hold his own in this race."

David moves to tower over Raul and me. His face is a sea of emotions: anger, hatred, hurt. I can't believe the poisonous stream of words that just poured out of me. I almost wish Raul had covered my mouth instead of sitting on my chest. At least Mother and Dad aren't part of this.

"Thanks for sitting on him, Raul," David says in a fake-polite voice. "Sorry you've been forced to be part of this *family dynamic*. And sorry you pulled the short straw on your own adoptive parents. But listen, if the two of you peel off from the race—if you defect from our team like I'm guessing you've been plotting to do— it doesn't spoil anything. We'll finish 'unranked.' How does that sound?"

His throat makes a noise like he's gathering spit to spray at me.

"David! Not another word from you!"

Mother's voice from the doorway makes all three of us swivel our heads. Her face is sheet white. Dad's is hurricane-force stormy, but he's hanging back to let her have her say. *How much have they heard?* My hollow chest tells me they've heard everything. What were we thinking, with these paper-thin walls? And why didn't they step in to stop us sooner? Yes, a part of me is glad they've heard it. But mostly I want to sink through the floor, or turn back time to before the moment I headed to the shower.

David, face tense, backs up a few steps.

"Mother, I—I'm sorry . . ." I begin as I sit up.

She seats herself slowly on David's bed, takes a moment to collect herself and then reaches out and squeezes my hand with determined force. "There's something I should explain, Andreo—should have told you long ago. After we adopted you, I was terrified some-one would come to take you back. Or that you'd have memories of your real—*er*, your birth mother. It's because you cried all the time. . . ."

"Screamed bloody murder, more like. Especially when your mother held you," Dad says, arms crossed but face losing its anger as he moves closer to Mother.

"You flailed your tiny arms like you were mad at me," Mother says, her voice a little choked. "Dad was the only one who could calm you. You went ballistic if I so much as touched you, maybe because you sensed my fear that someone would come to take you back. Eventually, I was afraid of touching you at all. I know I'm still not good at it. It has never meant I don't love you, Andreo."

"But . . . but I was only a baby. Don't all babies cry?"

"You cried way more than other babies," Dad asserts. "Even our friends who had kids said so. But we eventually learned to cope with you."

Mother releases my hand and a pained look comes over her face. "And now you've met her. . . ."

"I . . . I . . ."

"I heard what you said, Andreo. It's too late to take it back. And there's no time to discuss it now. The shuttle to the caving event arrives in fifteen minutes. But we will continue this discussion, I promise." She rises stiffly, like she's drained.

"Andreo and Raul," Dad's measured voice is saying, "do you want a time-out?"

A time-out? I picture myself as a little boy, sent to the corner for being bad.

"What I mean is, do you two want us to miss the

shuttle bus to the caving site and stay here until you sort out whatever it is you seem determined to sort out?"

I rankle at his use of "you two" rather than "us" or "our family."

"No," I say in a defeated tone.

"Yes," Raul says at the same time.

Everyone turns to stare at Raul.

"You need to make your decision before the shuttle comes," Mother says in a firm voice.

"Andreo and David," Dad says as he follows her to the door, "you've raised points that need to be addressed, along with issues such as stolen documents and pursuing potentially dangerous contacts behind our backs"—his eyes throw lightning bolts at me—"but this is neither the time nor the place."

It's never the time or place with you. Somehow, I manage not to say that aloud. They walk out of the room, Dad's arm around my mother. My chest is so tight that it feels ready to implode.

"We'll do the caving part," Raul calls after them, making my parents pause and turn around for a second. "Then we'll let you know."

CHAPTER FOURTEEN

I've heard of cults where, when a member breaks a rule, the others turn their backs on him, make him invisible to them. He's forced to leave because he basically no longer exists in their eyes.

I feel I've crossed the same sort of line here. As we squeeze aboard the back of a standing-room-only pickup truck—a vehicle that, judging from the smell, hauled a load of sheep shortly before it was hired to shuttle adventure racers to remote caves—Mother, Dad and David huddle together, talking, their backs to me. I know I should join them, ask forgiveness, but my emotions are so raw and tangled up, I'm unable to. So I push toward the far back corner where Raul is slumped.

From there, I observe my adoptive family. Mother looks like something a steamroller has knocked down and flattened. The one time her dazed eyes meet mine, they reveal the pain of a stabbing victim. I recall with a sinking feeling what she overheard: *Mother can't handle the fact I have another mother, a real mother. . . . I have met my birth mother and she is perfect. . . . My real father isn't unknown. And it wasn't my mother's choice to give me away.* My words have just made her worst nightmare come true, knifed her in the heart.

I see David wrap his arms around her. Guilt envelops me. Then there's Dad beside them, silent as stone: an unexploded grenade in a vehicle careening down a super-rutted road. Between my estranged family and me is a sea of fit bodies, excited chatter and the rank odor of unwashed sports clothes.

As we lurch over crater-size potholes that churn up my stomach, I'm reminded that, thanks to David's and my fight, none of us has had breakfast.

I watch scenery flash by. There is little vegetation. Just giant reddish rocks that look like they've fallen from outer space, and grass in sparse patches. On distant hills, I see other trucks full of adventure race teams heading to different sets of caves, some of the more than fifty in Torotoro National Park. Our huge shuddering Isuzu truck makes me feel like I'm in an earthquake. We bounce up and down steep rises, the truck barely clinging to the track as we round bends on overhangs. I'm sure I'm not the only one terrified that our vehicle will plunge over the edge at any moment.

"Have to tell you something, *mon*," Raul says.

I'm happy to turn my attention to my friend. "Like where you were this morning? Sneaking off with Maria, I'm guessing?"

"I was tailing you."

"Tailing me?"

"Someone has got to watch your back."

I shake my head in disbelief. "And what did you see?"

"Detective Colque had coffee with Dr. A while you were in the clinic."

"So?"

"After you and Detective Colque left, as soon as you were out of sight, a navy blue Jeep screeched up to the back door, and a young bearded guy with tattoos on his arms leaped out and half-pushed Vanessa inside."

I stare at him. "As in, kidnapped her?"

He studies a sheep turd on the floorboards in front of us. "*Nah*, probably just some impatient tough giving her a ride. Then I jogged after the truck." He coughs. "Got a lungful of dust for my effort. It sped out of town and climbed a steep hill—a hill with some caves that Maria and I explored yesterday."

"And?"

"I watched it for a while with my binoculars."

"So that's where the binoculars went," I say.

"They drove up to a shack. They got out and went inside."

"So you found out where she's staying. Whoop-de-do."

"Yeah, okay, so tell me what went down in the clinic."

I tell him the whole story. He avoids my eyes as I gush about my birth mother. But his head jerks up when I describe how evasive she was about who his own birth parents are.

"So she knows but won't tell," he says. His voice reveals both bitterness and hope. "Then we're not done with Torotoro."

My heart skips a beat. "What are you saying?"

"I'll do the caving part of the adventure race, because that's what I'm all about, and your family can't get through it without me. Then we're splitting from Team Family Dynamics."

"We?" I can't believe what I'm hearing.

"Andreo, you did great this morning. Standing up to David for once. And telling your parents like it is."

"Great?" my voice cracks. "I'm in total shit now. They hate me."

"They don't hate you. They're just in shock. But it's about time. And your family has given us permission to drop out."

"They have not given us permission to drop out!" I say in a low, urgent voice. "That was their twisted way of making us feel guilty and trying to keep us in line!"

"But we can pretend we have taken it as permission. We can take off. We have to see Vanessa again, don't you think?"

My head sinks into my hands; I'm totally muddled and torn. A part of me wants to elbow my way to my family. A part of me wants to leap out of the moving truck and charge up the hill to see my birth mother again. I picture her sipping tea in the shack, gently knitting with those long, elegant fingers, reminiscing on our conversation, wishing we'd had more time. And I can only imagine how much Raul wants to press Vanessa about his birth parents' identities.

"Gotta think" is all I say.

Where the truck unloads, there's an army of volunteers directing teams to different cave entrances. We're asked to leave our packs on one table and grab a white helmet with a light attached from another table.

"Remember," says a race volunteer on a megaphone, "this is not a timed part of the race, but a fun, skill-testing exercise. It's a diversion, a special feature you're all capable of doing because you completed your basic caving certification. When you finish, get your passports stamped and grab lunch from the food table. Then trucks will shuttle you down to where the bike vans wait, since the vans can't make it up to the caves. At the bike vans, you will be allowed to retrieve your bikes in a staggered fashion— according to when your team arrived in Torotoro."

Dad herds us to the cave entrance we've been assigned. Raul finally stops craning his neck to look for Maria and takes over as leader. I fall in place behind Raul; David, Mother and Dad follow us. We switch on our lights and descend slippery steps. Rock walls tower above us until we duck into a tunnel that eventually opens into a huge room. It's like walking into a dinosaur's mouth. Giant pointy teeth growing from both ceiling and floor look

ready to clench us tight. They're stalactites and stalag-
mites, of course: calcium drippings that have taken
more than a thousand years to form. The smell of mud
and calcium invades my nostrils.

Farther in, formations start resembling wax sculp-
tures. One looks like a Christmas tree and another like a
statue of the Virgin Mary. It's humid and warm, at first
a welcome break from the coolness outside. But soon I
begin to sweat. No one says a word as Raul leads us down
moist tunnels through which trickles of water flow.

Deeper into the cavern we go, a human chain moving
through a cavity that doubles as a shallow pond, then
breaking out into a high-ceilinged chamber over a brown
lagoon. It's now uncomfortably humid, almost like a sauna.

"Thought this was supposed to be fun," David
grumps. "Not my idea of 'a special feature.'"

"But it *is* fun, and it's fascinating because blind fish
live here," Raul says, like he's a guide. "Maria told me."

We direct our headlamps onto the muddy water, but
fail to see any sign of life. As we wade through the thigh-
high water to the other side, I hope that blind fish don't
bite. I also wonder how many times my birth father
guided here and whether Vanessa accompanied him
sometimes. I picture them wading through the water
hand in hand, giggling, tucking into a cavity for a picnic
and basking in the wonder and magic.

Raul leads us to a small tunnel on the far side that
works its way upward like a wormhole. We're on our

hands and knees, crawling along a passage, when I hear a shout from David.

"I hate this! I'm scared! Have to stop for a minute."

"Relax, David," Mother's muffled voice orders from way behind.

"Just keep crawling forward. It will widen in a moment," Dad adds.

"But I can't breathe!" comes my brother's panicked reply.

"Close your eyes until you calm down, honey," says Mother.

"Paste yourself to the wall, *mon*," Raul directs me, and, as we've done dozens of times before, we make like salamanders and do what for most would be impossible: squeeze past one another until I am in the lead and Raul is turned around and head-to-head with David.

"Keep going, Andreo," commands Raul, and I do, upward toward a hint of light, as I hear Raul speak gently and patiently to my brother to coax him out of his panic.

Emerging from the hole, I'm so blinded by the sun that I feel more than see a volunteer clasp my arm. "Your passport?" she asks.

"My dad's got it; he's coming up behind me in a minute." Fantastic as the caving was, I'm elated to be back in the fresh air.

"Okay, the line for the food table starts over there," she says.

I nod, exchange my helmet for my pack and position myself in the food line. I'm thinking about how famished I am when I hear a shout.

Shading my eyes, I glimpse a truck fully loaded with racers who've finished both their caving stint and lunches. As the truck's engine roars to life, I glimpse someone sprinting toward it—Raul. A forest of strong arms reaches out to lift him and his pack over the tailgate as the truck begins moving. Then I hear my name being called from two directions.

Mother, Dad and David are hailing me as they walk from the cave exit toward the food line. But as I swivel my head, I see Raul standing in the truck, waving his arms at me, screaming, "Now, Andreo! Now!"

My feet decide for me. They run toward the truck, then lift off the ground like I'm doing a pole-vault move. The same forest of arms hauls me aboard just as the driver guns it.

"Way to go, *mon.*" Raul slaps me on the back as the swerving truck pitches us into our fellow occupants. I scramble up and stare at the sight of my mother, running with arms outstretched, shouting something over and over, words becoming so faint that I can barely make them out.

"Andreo, Andreo, my son. Don't you know how much I love you?"

Fifteen minutes later, when the truck reaches the bike van, a burly volunteer refuses to release our bikes to us.

"Need your passport and the rest of your team members," he says. "Then we will inform you of your approved start time."

"Not if we're going unranked," Raul says.

The guy raises an eyebrow.

"We're dropping out. The rest of our team will be here to continue shortly," I say, my throat tight. *Will the volunteer fall for it? Will my family?* The guy shrugs and scribbles in his notebook. Before he can change his mind, we pull our bikes out of the van, me pausing long enough to attach the note I've written during the bumpy ride to Dad's bike crossbar with a piece of duct tape from my pack. Then we take off north toward Cochabamba, waiting till we're out of the volunteer's sight before we peel off the road and head east instead, me drafting Raul on a dusty off-road dash.

CHAPTER FIFTEEN

"What'd you write in the note?" Raul asks as we lie on dry, prickly grass behind a stout rock formation, drinking the last dregs of our water and sharing an energy bar between us.

"That we're biking to Cochabamba ahead of them to finish getting information there that we still want regarding our adoptions."

"Smart thinking. They'll spend hours figuring they will catch up with us."

"And I said that we appreciate their permission to take some time off and let the team go to unranked."

"*Mmmm.* Your dad's going to be majorly pissed."

I hang my head. "Yeah, even David's going to be amazed by us taking off." I refuse to contemplate how my adoptive mother will react. "I also said we'll meet them at the hotel after they finish the race."

Raul nods. "It'll take them two days to get to the official finish line in Cochabamba." He drains his hydration pack, then removes it to try and shake some last droplets into his mouth. "Cochabamba. Hotel. Hot tub. Food. We're nuts, *mon*."

"Yeah, I should've grabbed some sandwiches from the food table on the way to the truck."

"Then you'd've missed the truck."

"True. Was that a cool move or what, getting on board at the last second?" I try to banish the image of my mother chasing us. I'll be reunited with them in Cochabamba in two days; we'll talk then and make things right somehow. Maybe Raul is correct: It is not so much that they hate me as that they're in shock.

Truth is, though, a part of me is high on having taken a stand and run away. All my life I've lived by their rules, lived in fear of getting them angry or hurting my mother by mentioning the *A* word. All my life I've lived under the shadow of David. Now I've waved the adoption issue in their faces, and no one can make me take it back. No one can take away the dreamlike meeting with my beautiful birth mother, or the victory of finally discovering who my birth father is. He was a guide, a hero, someone admired around here. My real father, my bloodline. It's all heady information, and it has given me permission to chase my own dreams and break away from the restrictions of theirs. They're not my real family! They can't tell me what to do!

I leap up. The air is incredibly fresh up here, and the rugged rocks have a stark beauty all their own. I feel strong and exhilarated and ready to meet Vanessa—*er*,

Mom—again. "Come on. How far to Mom's house?" I ask.

Raul gives me a strange look. Then we stand, shoulder our packs and get back on our bikes. Like Butch Cassidy and the Sundance Kid—the famous outlaws who rode their horses with the law in hot pursuit through this very landscape, the ones they made the movie about— we carry on. For more than an hour we navigate the dry, rocky terrain, a series of striped sedimentary hills broken only by clumps of grass, the occasional stubby bush and fortresslike stone formations on hilltops.

Twice we divert to climb down gullies and fill our hydration packs from streams trickling between four-story-tall boulders. Such rivulets feel like secret trails squeezed between erect buildings. Awed by these mini-canyons, their birdsong and occasional flowers, we walk along, feeling like cowboys strolling down a ghost town's main street, before climbing back up gaps between the rock faces to our bicycles.

Raul punctures and patches his tires twice; I curse as I'm forced to do the same. More than once, we have to dismount and carry our bikes over un-navigable stretches of reddish stones. Finally, Raul slows and points up a particularly steep hill on the outskirts of Torotoro. He pulls out the binoculars. "Up there."

We take turns looking through them. All I can see is a blue Jeep in front of a crude shack. Then a man appears in the doorway, looks about and lights a cigar.

"There's a man up there. A fat one," I say.

Raul grabs the binoculars and focuses them. I hear him draw in his breath. "Pay dirt," he says. "Keep down."

"*Huh?*"

"That, my friend, is Hugo Vargas. I've seen enough Internet photos of him that I'd lay money on it."

I take the binoculars back and stare. Unlike Raul, I've paid little attention to photos of the alleged black-market gang kingpin. As I zoom in on the man's pencil-thin mustache, I feel panic squeeze my chest.

"Raul, if she's in there too, it means that tattooed guy you saw at the Torotoro doctor's clinic really did kidnap her—captured her to take her to Vargas."

Raul says nothing.

"Raul? Do you hear me? We have to rescue her."

"Andreo, if she's kidnapped, we go to the police. We—do—not—rescue—her. Is that clear?"

I start to jump up, but he pulls me down so fast I stub my chin on a rock.

"Police?" I question. "This guy Vargas might take her off somewhere before we can get police up there! But we—you and I—can sneak up there now, Raul, and break her out somehow!"

Raul won't meet my eyes, which makes me want to punch him between his.

"Okay, Andreo, here's my suggestion. We phone Detective Colque. It's not far into town. He may not have left Torotoro yet, and he'll know what to do."

Raul waits. I want to argue, but a glance toward town

makes me realize it won't take long to get to a phone. If Detective Colque doesn't answer or has left town, I'll go back up the hill myself if I have to.

"Okay, let's go," I agree, lowering the binoculars. "Mr. Vargas has gone back inside."

We pick up our bikes and pump to town. We slip into the Internet café and fish coins from our pockets for the call. Raul stands in the doorway staring toward the hill and drumming his fingers annoyingly as I press my ear to the receiver.

"*Hola?*" a voice crackles over the phone line.

"Detective Colque! *Phew!*"

"Andreo? I thought you'd be done with caving and on the road to Cochabamba by now. What's going on?"

I lower my voice to a husky whisper and tell him how Raul and I defected because we wanted to talk to my birth mother once again, and how my parents think we're biking to Cochabamba ahead of them. I tell him of sighting Vargas, lowering my excited voice when I see Raul signaling me to keep it down. *Is he imagining that Vargas has spies in the Internet café?*

There's a moment of silence as Detective Colque takes this in, then the usual enthusiasm in his voice. "This is a major scoop, Andreo. I told you he skipped bail, didn't I? There's a search on for him. He'd never hurt Vanessa, Andreo—for sure he wouldn't—but if he saw her talking to you the other morning, he might have wanted to question her.

"In any case, if you really have located Hugo Vargas, we have to notify the police. It'll be a feather in my cap— and yours—if they get him as a result. Okay, this is really lucky timing because I'm still in Torotoro; I was just about to head out of town. You're at the Internet café? I'll swing by in five minutes; you can load your bikes into the back of my truck. Does that work for you?"

"Perfect!" I slam down the phone and grin at my accomplice. Good as his word, the detective swings by in a shiny red 4x4 within five minutes. We head to the lookout point. Since Detective Colque has a pair of binoculars too, we share the two among the three of us.

"Jeep's gone," Raul cries.

I zoom in and feel my heart fall from my throat to my stomach. "Detective, can we go up there? The police are taking too long."

"I didn't phone the police," the detective says. "I felt I needed to make positive visual identification before I did that."

"Then we've let him escape!" I say, distressed.

"But maybe Vanessa is still there?" Raul suggests.

"I'm willing to drive up to see," the detective says cautiously, "if you two promise to stay in the truck when we get there."

We agree, slide down in our seats and tolerate the lurching ride up the winding road. Behind us, a trail of dust rises into the noon sky. Not far from the shack, the road ends. He pulls to a stop. I stare. It's a hut with a corrugated tin roof, iron bars over the only window, a deadbolt pulled into place on the outside of the door and no yard or fence—just gravel and a nearby outhouse.

"Someone would actually live here?" I say.

The detective shrugs. "Probably a miner's supply hut back in its day."

We sit and observe it for a moment. There's no sound up here but the whistle of a low wind. I jump at the squeak of the detective pulling on the hand brake.

"Stay here, as we agreed," Detective Colque says and opens his door cautiously.

My body tenses as he walks around the outside of the shack, pausing at the dirty window to cup his hands and peer in. After he does two full circles around the building, we watch him pull open the dead bolt of the hut's door and look inside.

A moment later, he steps outside again, closes the door, pushes the dead bolt back and strolls to the truck.

"Nothing and no one."

Before I can answer, Raul opens his door and leaps out. He runs to the shack and wrenches the front door open, prompting me to jump out and run after him. Detective Colque is on my heels.

Inside, the shack doesn't look like something anyone would live in. An empty, overturned dynamite box and bench for table and chairs, a threadbare quilt on a rusty iron bed with a thin mattress, and no running water: just a large plastic jug perched on a linoleum counter scarred with cigarette burns beside a dented aluminum sink. Except for three teacups in the sink, a few tins of food in one cupboard and Coca-Cola bottles filled with the local brew *chicha*, there's little sign anyone has been here. It looks like an abandoned shack someone has hung out in briefly. It smells of cigar smoke, mold—and rose perfume, unless I'm imagining that. Anyway, she's not here, not a captive locked inside as I'd feared.

"You're sure this is the right place?" Detective Colque asks, scratching his chin.

"Of course we are," Raul says.

"But how sure are you it was Hugo Vargas?"

"I just think it was," my friend says, sounding less confident.

"A blue Jeep, you said. Do you have the license plate number?"

Raul shakes his head and I, too, want to kick myself for not thinking of that.

"Well, we seem to have missed whoever it was, but the police—"

"Whom you never called . . . ," Raul interrupts.

I throw him a look of surprise for his rudeness, but Detective Colque doesn't seem to notice.

"I will tell the police to keep an eye on it, and around town, just in case. We'll catch him. He must know his hours as a free man are numbered." The detective sounds as bummed out as I feel. "So what now?" he asks. "Want a lift back to Cochabamba with your bikes?" Neither

Raul nor I reply. I have no idea what I want. But facing my parents at the finish line isn't top of my list.

"Thanks, detective, but we want to bike," says Raul. "It's what we signed on for, even if we have let our team get ahead of us. Anyway, I'm for getting some food before we get back on the road. What about you, Andreo?"

"Starving."

"Good lads. Well, I'll drop you in town, then, and I'll see you back in the big city in two days. I guess you won't have e-mail access, but in an emergency, definitely phone again. Enjoy your ride."

CHAPTER SIXTEEN

Back in town, we use some of our emergency money to buy food and water before hopping on our bikes and heading out. I'm in some kind of mental fog, following Raul because he seems to be decisive about where we're going. I tell myself that if Vanessa was ever in that cabin, it was only briefly, and Raul and I may have been completely wrong about seeing Hugo Vargas.

Anyway, what right did we have to spy on my birth mother or try to see her again? I can e-mail her through Detective Colque; maybe she'll eventually soften and tell us who Raul's parents are, if she even knows. Maybe it is time to head back to Cochabamba and face my parents.

My thoughts are interrupted when Raul pulls off the main road.

"I want to go to the Matrimonial Cave," he states.

"You and Maria getting married?"

"*Ha-ha.*"

"It'll take too long, Raul. We need to get to Cochabamba."

"It's only a few minutes away, Andreo. You really have to see it. Trust me. Please?"

I frown, then shrug. "Okay, if it's that special. But only for a few minutes."

"I promise."

At the Matrimonial Cave, a boy half-dozing in the shade of a bush looks surprised to see us pull up on bikes. Judging from the size of the parking lot, he is more used to tour buses disgorging fifty customers at a time. I don't like the way his eyes latch on to our sturdy mountain bikes. He rises slowly, yawns and shakes a can of coins at us. We pay the fee he asks and wander into the cave, wheeling our bikes with us. Instantly, the coolness and grandeur of the cathedral-like space mesmerize me. We're the only visitors, and I wander around the echoey expanse in a happy trance, staring up at the vaulted ceilings. Among the spectacular rock formations are some that look like choir stalls, maybe even angels. A high-up section of stalactites definitely resembles a pipe organ.

Raul, who has seen it all before, heads directly to a moist wall in the back of the cave, where a stack of folding chairs looks ready for duty should a bride, groom and congregation arrive.

"Where are you going?" the guard boy asks as Raul stops in front of a locked cupboard beside the chairs.

"I want to see the registry of everyone married in this cave," Raul says in Spanish. "Is it in this cupboard?"

"Raul, what are you up to?" I demand.

"It's not for the public," the boy barks.

Raul pulls out a wad of our emergency money. The boy's eyes grow large as Raul extends a stack of bills and asks, "Enough?"

"Raul—"

"I'll explain in a minute," he says casually.

The boy grabs the money from Raul's outstretched palm. He fishes a key from a cord around his neck, opens the cupboard and produces a large book filled with yellowed, mildewed, smudged pages.

Raul turns the pages rapidly, his finger running down columns of dates. "You have other, older books?" he asks eventually.

The boy's eyes narrow, but he drags out a stack from the bottom of the cupboard. Raul digs through until he finds the one he wants, then flips through it methodically. Slowly, almost reluctantly, he hands it to me, his finger pressed to a particular line.

"Vanessa Gutierrez and Hugo Vargas," I read in disbelief. The date recorded is roughly a year after I was born. The witness is Dr. Zacharie Akumuntu.

A roaring fills my ears. I slam the book shut, which sends dust flying up my nostrils, and shove it back in the arms of the boy.

"You pulled me up here because you suspected this?" I accuse my friend.

"Sorry, Andreo," he replies softly. "I was afraid you wouldn't come if I told you what I was up to."

"Damn right I wouldn't have!" Shaking with rage and confusion, I flee from the cave, from Raul, from everything to do with the Matrimonial Cave, dragging my bike with me. I swing my leg over the crossbar, grip my handlebars and take off, almost mowing down a newly arrived flood of tourists coming off a bus in the parking lot.

Raul is shouting, but I can outride him. I can outride my thoughts, my family—birth and adoptive—and myself.

I don't know how far I ride before a rock punctures my tire. After dismounting, I kick my bike, cursing, then sink to the dusty, empty road and feel hot salty tears spill down my cheeks. I curl into a ball and let myself sob as if I were a little kid. There's no one anywhere near to see or hear me. Only dry, desolate, rocky terrain.

All sense of time disappears under the graying early-afternoon sky. When I'm finally spent, my face a mess of sodden dust, I dig in my pack for some food. Beef jerky goes down with a swill of bottled water. Staring at a swarming anthill near my feet, wondering where I am, I tug out the map, smooth it on the ground and look at it blankly. Some navigator. I'm lost. Inside and out.

"We're due west of the Matrimonial Cave," says a voice behind me. "And just northwest of town."

I take a deep breath and refuse to turn around. He drops down beside me.

"Sorry, *mon*."

My teeth grit together. *How dare he follow me!*

"Doesn't mean they're still married. Doesn't mean anything," I say defiantly.

He shakes his head. "Time to get real, Andreo."

"They could've divorced years ago. She wouldn't stay with a jerk like that. Maybe they hadn't seen each other in ages and he brought her up to that shack to question her after she met with me, just like Colque said. Maybe it's all my fault for meeting with her."

"You're still clinging to the fairy-tale birth-mother thing."

I pick up a nearby stone and aim it at him. He doesn't flinch.

"You just had to haul me there, didn't you? You couldn't stand for me to be happy when you never got to meet yours."

"Oh, so now it's all my fault."

"For all I know, you scribbled that marriage entry into the stupid book when you and Maria were running around the cave yesterday."

"Come off it, *mon.* You're cracking up." Raul rises, his face drained of sympathy. "It's time for us to head back to Cochabamba, Andreo. You know the truth now, and your parents will be worrying soon."

"My parents." I spit into the dirt. "They're not my parents. David's not my brother. They're a lousy family."

"You don't know anything about lousy families." His tone holds a warning, but I don't care.

"We could stay here together, Raul. You said yourself that your family sucks and there's no point going home."

"Yeah, and I didn't mean it, just like you don't mean what you're saying now. Got some water, by the way? My hydration pack punctured when I fell off my bike following you here."

I let him drink from mine. "You could stay here with Maria. We could stay here together. This is Bolivia, our real home."

"Andreo, pull yourself together and let's get biking. We have to get to Cochabamba before your parents panic and call the police on us."

"*You* go!" I shout. "Get out of my face! It's none of your business what I do!"

Raul hesitates, then shakes his head, mounts his bike and rides away, heading north. His dust trail swirls and rises to meet blackening clouds. I look down and kick the anthill till its residents swarm in confusion, their home a mess.

I wipe my sleeve across my face and force myself to replay my meeting with Vanessa. I try to cling to the memory of the rose perfume, silken hair and long embrace. I hear her soft voice: *I've waited for this a very long time* and *Call me Mom.*

Then I flash back to something Maria's grandmother said: *She was a quiet girl, always did what she was told.*

Had Vargas told her what to say to me? I remember the way Vanessa urged me to tell her about myself. *What did*

I learn about her? Almost nothing. She works as a secretary for an international firm. . . .

"No way," I say aloud, crushing a light brown, medium-size ant that has crawled up my shin and bitten me. The international firm she works for is Vargas's black-market business. So Raul had figured out that that was a possibility but was right that I'd never have accepted it without seeing the documents in the Matrimonial Cave.

Yes, I'm married. Very happily. Not to your father. Her glowing face as she said that looms in my mind; the memory stings like my ant bite. Married happily to a scumbag. A criminal on the run. To the person who took her in when she had no one and helped sell her baby. Me.

After Vanessa had you, Ardillita had said, *she stayed on to help the housemother. Nowhere else to go but the streets, I suppose. She was good to me.*

I picture my first glimpse of Vanessa in the clinic: her high heels, diamond earrings and elegant sweater. Her nervous smile and the way she became distant when I asked about Raul's parents. Of course she knows who Raul's birth parents are! She helped arrange the adoption, profited from it. And from the other 598 babies.

I crush another ant. I stand and stomp on as many as I can, destroying the last bits of their hill in the process.

Why did she agree to meet with me at all? The answer comes all too quickly: Ardillita spotted her in town and tipped me off. I told Detective Colque, and he called Dr. A to try and locate her for me.

I step away from the anthill. Dr. A has probably been referring girls in trouble to Vargas all along, including Vanessa when she was seventeen. Of course, Vargas could pay lots of different village doctors for referrals. And hadn't my outburst to his receptionist brought Dr. A away from his lunch break pretty damn fast? He knew who I was instantly.

So Dr. A notified Vargas, whom he knew to be hiding out in Torotoro, in the shack on the hill. Vargas didn't want Colque to make the connection between himself and Vanessa, and didn't want Raul and me to figure out where Vanessa was staying. So Vargas persuaded Vanessa—his *wife* Vanessa, I think bitterly—to meet me at the clinic and give me what I wanted, hoping I'd be satisfied and carry on with the adventure race and get out of the country, out of his hair. And hoping that would get Colque out of Torotoro and back to Cochabamba too, to cool his chances of finding out where Vargas really was.

I ease my aching head into my hands. All my life I've dreamed about my birth mother. I created a fantasy birth mother; Raul is right about that. But can I dismantle her in a day?

Her words to me may or may not have been genuine, but in the sixteen years since she had me, she has helped Vargas sell babies for profit. She married him by choice; she opted to become his criminal accomplice. Between them, they've messed up the lives of 600 innocent babies and taken advantage of tons of teenage girls and

trusting couples. I owe her nothing; all I can do to coun-
teract the ugliness of the truth I've just uncovered is to
help shut down this ring now. Yes—I stand up and step
away from the homeless ants already desperately running in circles to build anew—that is my new mission
before I leave Bolivia.

A cold drop of rain plops on my head. I look up. The
storm clouds are ready to spill. Soon I'm getting splat-
tered big-time. Time to move, but where am I going?
To town to notify Detective Colque, I decide. Can I
turn in my own birth mother along with Vargas? If she
is innocent, I reason, the police will sort it out. If she's
not, I will have done the right thing.

I fix the flat tire and pedal hard in the pounding rain.
It takes an hour to reach the Internet café, where I pay
to use the phone. My hand is so wet I can barely grip
the receiver, but Colque doesn't answer anyway. When
a recording suggests leaving a message, I blurt out
something about the Matrimonial Cave revealing the
Vargas/Vanessa connection and urge him to relay that
to the police. Then I say Raul and I are finally heading
back to Cochabamba.

I come out of the Internet café shaking all over. If
Colque's not available, I should notify the local police
myself. Colque said he'd tell them to keep an eye on the
shack, but since he wasn't convinced it was Vargas, maybe
he never bothered.

I push my bike up wet, cobbled streets toward the

police station, which turns out to be a small, drab, stucco building with chipped roof tiles. I'm still well down the street from it when I see two men come out of the door and pause to chat. I step back into the shadows of a building. The tall, strongly built man looks familiar. Slowly, I recognize him as the guy who introduced us to Maria at the start of the race: Ricardo Ferreira, Cochabamba police chief. *What's he doing in Torotoro?* My taut chest relaxes: He's Colque's boss, obviously, following up on a call from the detective and finally closing in on Vargas. The other guy, dressed in a similar uniform, must be the local sheriff. Just as I decide to move forward and introduce myself, they spin around to paste a poster up on the police notice board. I squint to see what it's about. *Yes!* I smile.

"WANTED: HUGO VARGAS."

I'd recognize his picture anywhere by now: the thin mustache, beady eyes and black fedora. Then I see the men paste another poster up. I draw back into the shadows in horror. *What?* This one features Raul and me!

CHAPTER SEVENTEEN

The hill is steeper than it looks. As I pump my bike pedals, my breath comes in gasps, even though I'm in super shape. Darkness is falling as fast as the rain. I had two choices back there: turn myself in to the police and get a free ride back to Cochabamba in a police cruiser, ready to face my parents' fury and rejection. Or wheel away at high speed. Without taking time to think it through, I panicked and did the second.

My parents should be less than halfway to Cochabamba by now; they should still be trying to catch up with Raul and me. Yet they somehow know we ditched the race entirely, and now they've handed our photos to the police.

Gritting my teeth, I pedal harder. I feel so guilty, muddled and torn that all I'm aware of is a need to clear my head. Biking in the rain is usually good for that.

I'm not really staying in Bolivia. That was just foolish talk. I shouldn't have blown Raul off like that, but he'll forgive me. Just needed some space and time.

Why am I biking up the hill toward the stupid shack? I want to see if anyone's there. Maybe I'm clinging to the hope that Vanessa has nothing more to do with Vargas. Maybe I want to be a hero and free her if he is holding her there. Or maybe I want to witness the two of them captured by the police, tipped off by my phone call to Colque. Regardless, I'm just going to look from a distance, then speed back down the hill, turn myself in and make sure the police shut down Vargas's operation. It's getting too late to catch up with Raul by bike now, let alone with my adoptive parents.

Darkness has fully descended as I draw near the place. The rain batters the corrugated tin roof in a steady drumbeat. There's no Jeep parked outside, which means Tattoo Guy is off somewhere. The dead bolt is off; she hasn't been locked up here. But a light inside the shack silhouettes a lone figure. I edge closer, then look back down the road, expecting Police Chief Ferreira any moment. I tell myself not to go closer. But the light draws me forward until I'm feet from the barred window. I smile. It's Vanessa.

She is seated on a rough-hewn bench that serves as the shack's only seating. There's a steaming cup of tea on the box-table beside her. Her long, unbraided hair falls over her delicate shoulders. She's wearing a lacy blue sweater. Flashy sapphire earrings wink at me. They match the sturdy, blue man's hat she is knitting. She's bent studiously over her work, her long eyelashes blinking as her needles complete each stitch.

She's so beautiful I feel my breath catch. The soft light reveals a freshly cleaned kitchen and vase of marigolds on the table. There's no one else about. A gentle force moves me toward the door; I'm startled to find myself turning the doorknob.

"Mom," I say quietly.

Her head jerks up. She drops her knitting. Surprise then fear flood her face. She rises.

"Andreo! What are you doing here? I don't know how you found me, but you have to leave this instant!"

"I just wanted to see you again," I say, reluctantly snapping out of my dreamlike state. It's as if she has tossed ice water in my face.

"Get out!" she says in a shrill voice I never imagined she could have. "For your own safety, boy, run!"

Boy? My face hardens and I pull the next words out of a cold place in my constricted heart. "So our entire meeting was fake, was it? Did Vargas tell you everything to say and do? You hugged me just to hide your face, didn't you?"

Her mouth comes unhinged in a less-than-attractive fashion. "If I say yes, will you go?" It sounds like a desperate plea. She moves her arms like she's trying to sweep me out the door.

"I'll go when you tell me the truth." I plant my feet so firmly that nothing and no one can move them. "I know you're married to Hugo Vargas."

Her face drains of color at this.

"We found the registry book at the Matrimonial Cave. And I know he has jumped bail and the police are closing in. So you're obviously on the run with him."

She stumbles backward and lowers herself uneasily to the bench. "Ask your questions, Andreo. It's your funeral." Her tone has gone cold. The hurt all but crushes me. Even so, I struggle to stay composed.

"Did Hugo tell you everything to say and do?"

"More or less." Her voice wavers a little.

"Was any of it true?"

She hesitates. "Yes."

"My birth father?"

"Marcelo Quispe, like I told you." Her eyes hold mine steadily, revealing sadness for an instant. It's a matter-of-fact tone tinged with impatience, like we aren't talking about something of earth-shattering importance in my life.

"You have other children?"

"No."

I preferred her earlier answer: *I've not been blessed that way. Which may be why I've thought of you so much over the years.*

"Who's the guy with the tattoos?"

"Jorge, our guard."

"You work for Vargas."

"Obviously." Her chin lifts and her features convert to a defiant stare.

"You live in Cochabamba?"

"We did, but we're leaving tonight—leaving Bolivia."

That's what *she* thinks. I wonder again what's taking the police so long. "Where's Vargas?"

Her hands twist in her lap. "Using the outhouse, outside." That gets my attention. My body tenses and I move toward the door. But I have one more question.

"Who are Raul's parents?"

The opening door slams into my backside. A fat, mustached man in a dripping black raincoat walks in calmly and removes his fedora. He smiles genially and extends his hand. "Andreo Gutierrez. So nice to meet you again after all these years."

I take a step back. He and I both know that his bulk easily prevents any escape. He smells of stale cigar smoke and time in an outhouse. My heart is racing, but I make a concerted effort to show no fear. Vanessa moves to stand beside him. The contrast between the fat, ugly man and striking, trim woman couldn't be starker. And now both are blocking my exit.

"You were my first, you know." Vargas snakes a fleshy arm around my birth mother's waist. I watch her body relax. "Yes, you and Vanessa were a most special gift: the start of a very successful business and a most satisfying life." He caresses Vanessa's hair; her responding smile makes me clench my teeth.

I feel blood running through my veins, as if the fantasy I've held on to for all these years is being pushed out by a spontaneous blood transfusion.

"Andreo, you're a foolish, foolish boy." He wags his finger like a kindergarten teacher chastising a student. "Trying to pursue a woman who never indicated she wanted to be pursued. Snooping beyond any safe or sensible point. Abandoning your adoptive parents and the race you came for, according to one of my race-volunteer contacts," he tsk-tsks me. "What were you hoping to accomplish this evening, anyway, may I ask?"

My tongue is stuck to the roof of my mouth. He shakes his head dramatically and sighs. "This very moment, you could be nearing your finish line. Finishing your adventure race in a respectable time, with a respectable family. A family who paid a pretty penny to acquire you." A cracked smile spreads across his jowly face.

"I didn't want to go through with our meeting," Vanessa tells me quietly, apologetically. "I begged Hugo not to make me. . . ."

"You begged not to meet your own son?"

She falls silent and stares at the floor.

"You sell human beings," I say, drawing myself up and addressing both of them with the full strength of my voice. "You sell babies, forgetting that they grow up! They grow up wondering who their real parents are, why they were torn away and what they did wrong to make their parents reject them. Did you ever think of that? Do you care about anything but the money?" I don't wait for an answer. "You tell adoptive parents anything they want to hear, don't you? You work with doctors all over to find teenage girls as desperate as you once were"—I jab my finger at Vanessa. "You tell them lies, anything to get their babies, anything to—"

"Andreo, Andreo," comes Vargas's voice, exaggerating patience. "You're focused on only one side of this. What about the couples brokenhearted over their inability to have a family? Young men and women whose arms ache to hold a baby? People willing to pay anything, do anything, ignore all such questions and issues? We are matchmakers, Andreo. We take babies that birth mothers are unable to cope with and give childless couples joy. It's a joy we witness with every match, a happiness you can't even imagine."

My birth mother is nodding, looking at me hopefully. I'm too stunned to reply.

"Yes, the children may grow up wondering at times," Vargas continues, "but their lives are much, much richer for the transfer. They may wonder about the real story, but it's almost always a sad story. A tragic story. A story whose ending we can change."

His eyes are bright. He's smiling like someone high on something. His hands are moving like an actor delivering Academy Award–winning lines. He's a zealot who actually believes he's some kind of do-gooder!

"Vanessa and I, we're proud of what we do. If you could see the looks on the faces of the couples who adopt, you'd understand. Your parents, they were my first clients. All they wanted was a child to love and care for. A boy to raise with all the love and wisdom and resources they had. Have they done a good job, Andreo? I think so. I was there when you were handed over. The gratitude on their faces was—"

He stops, almost choked up. Vanessa squeezes his hand. The photo of my smiling parents holding me outside Vargas's office sixteen years ago forces itself upon me. But my silence lasts only a second.

"You're a criminal, the worst kind," I bark, pulling all my courage together. "A black-market baby stealer. The records of all the babies you sold—if you even kept records—I suppose you think you can carry them out of the country with you, so none of us will ever be able to . . ."

Now Vargas is laughing. He walks across the room and pulls a suitcase out from under the bed: an expensive, red-leather suitcase with a strap around its middle secured by a heavy lock. He releases the lock and lifts out a yellow spiral notebook that itself has a lock. I realize that only Vanessa is now between me and the door, but there's no way I'm dashing out without at least trying to get that notebook. He lifts the tome and waves it at me as Vanessa's nervous eyes flit from him to me. "Yes, Andreo, it's going with me. Or maybe I'll burn it tonight. We were just trying to decide that."

I lunge across the room and grab for it, but he easily pulls it out of my reach and, with a deft move of his right knee, knocks me to the floor. I scramble up and back away from him toward Vanessa, toward the door. *Fine. I'll let the police take it.* It's time for me to get out while I can.

"You're both losers," I say as a parting shot. This launches Vargas into a big belly laugh.

I stride toward the door and for a split second, I think they are going to let me go. But as I yank it open, there's Tattoo Man—Jorge—standing in the doorway, rain-soaked and scowling. One signal from Vargas and the guard's thick arms wrap around me, one of his elbows locking around my neck.

First I raise my hands to wrestle with the mass of muscle. Then I attempt to sink my teeth into an arm and kick as hard as I can. My nose scrunches up at the reek of beer and body odor. Jorge merely chuckles as he flops me chin-first onto the ground and holds me there with his boot like a cat playing with a mouse.

I'm still hoping desperately for the sound of a police siren. I left that message on Colque's phone an hour ago. Instead, I'm forced to listen as Vargas, Vanessa and Jorge talk in rapid-fire Spanish. I catch the words "posters" and "leave now." Eventually, Vargas walks calmly to his and Vanessa's suitcase, drops the notebook into it and locks the case with a flourish. Jorge starts gathering tins of food from the cupboards and stuffing bottles of *chicha* into a shoulder bag with great care. Vanessa fills some bottles of water from the container on the counter while gazing sadly at the vase of marigolds, as if she hates to leave them behind. *She's more reluctant to leave the flowers behind than to see the last of her only son*, I think bitterly.

Moments later, she nods her readiness at Vargas. Jorge sneers at me as he holds the door open for the couple.

"Don't worry, Andreo," Vargas says. "Someone will find you by the time we've crossed the border. By the way, I am glad we placed you with a good family. I just wish they'd kept you in Canada."

Vanessa gathers up her knitting. "Good-bye, Andreo," she says softly, and pulls the door shut soundlessly. I jump at the sound of the dead bolt outside sliding into place.

CHAPTER EIGHTEEN

I try the door—locked solidly—and rattle the iron bars on the window. I search desperately for a hole or weakness somewhere, a possible way out. Nothing. Then I sink onto the bed and take some deep breaths to unchoke myself.

Was it really only six o'clock this morning that I met Vanessa for the very first time, a meeting that turned out to be too good to be true? I try to wrap my mind around all that has happened since then: the big blowup with my family, the caving event, Raul's and my defection, our sighting of Vargas and his disappearance from this shack before Colque got us up the hill. The Matrimonial Cave discovery and then, regrettably, my fight with Raul. Witnessing the WANTED posters going up: Vargas's and ours side by side. *How ironic was that?*

If I'd hung around any longer outside the police station, would I have seen Vanessa's photo added? Maybe they're not on to her yet. Then, the day's stupidest decision of all: biking up the hill and entering this miserable hut on my own. And now here I am, a prisoner as the fugitives escape. And no one has a clue where I am.

My shoulders slump; my eyes sting. Worst of all, Vargas's words keep slapping me in the face: *Vanessa and I, we're proud of what we do. If you could see the looks on the faces of the couples who adopt. . . . All they wanted was a child to love and care for.*

Someone to love till David came along, I try to tell myself, but the notion feels petty, childish, ridiculous. Yes, they love me too. They don't really mean to favor David; maybe they don't know they're doing it. *Why have I never admitted that before? And where is my adoptive family at the moment? Did they abandon the race when they realized I double-crossed them?* I didn't mean for them to miss out on the finish. I thought that was what they wanted most. I have no idea how they figured out Raul and I weren't on the road ahead of them, but they acted on it right away. Contacted police. Supplied photos. Are probably crazed with worry and fear for us. *What have I done?*

If I get out of this shack, I promise myself, I'll make it up to them. I'll make it up to David too—I'll stop being jealous of him, stop treating him like shit. Even if he doesn't return the favor. I'll make my mother hug me. I'm bigger than her. I smile at that thought. She's not dainty, pretty and fashionable like my birth mother; she's strong and reliable—in every respect except her fear of losing me to unknown birth parents. I'm strong and reliable like her, and like Dad, right? I'll hug her till she can't remember when we didn't.

My throat closes up again. My eyes sting.

"Well, well, didn't you screw up?"

I blink. Is that really Raul standing dripping wet in front of me, the door wide open, a curtain of rain behind him?

"Raul!" I jump up to hug him. I've never been so happy to see anyone in my life. He tolerates a quick embrace.

He lowers his pack to the floor, where it creates a puddle.

"Where'd you come from? Why are you here?" I ask.

"Followed you—into town and then up here."

I stare at him. "Dude, you gotta get a life."

He barely cracks a smile, then starts opening cupboards looking for food. He tosses a can of sardines and two bottles of *chicha* that Jorge managed to miss into his pack.

"They took off, all three of them, in the Jeep," I tell him.

"I know, and ran out of gas five minutes later." He smirks and crosses his arms.

"You siphoned their gas?"

"Isn't that what tubes from punctured hydration packs are for? Where were they heading, anyway?"

"Across the border. Out of Bolivia."

"Which border?"

I blanch and shrug. East or west, Brazil or Chile, I hadn't even thought to wonder. "She wouldn't have told me if I'd asked, anyway. So, are they walking to town? Or heading back here?" I glance nervously at the door.

"They headed west, through thick brush, with a

flashlight. I learned some new Spanish cuss words following them. They kept trying to phone someone, I suppose to come get them, but I don't think they ever got through. They've settled themselves into a big, dry cave a twenty-minute walk from here. Now let's get out of this place before they change their minds about their evening's accommodation."

We exit the shack hurriedly, slipping the dead-bolt into place.

"Raul, we can't just let them get away."

"Leave them to the police. The Jeep guy has a gun. We're in over our heads, Andreo. You're lucky they didn't hurt you. Where's your bike and pack? I'll race you to the police station."

I walk over to retrieve my pack and bike from where I'd hidden them. I clamp my helmet on my head and flick on its light. It illuminates Raul's impatient face, where he waits on his bike. "Raul, they've got a registry of all the babies they ever sold."

I watch his jaw work back and forth. "Is that why you went into the shack?"

I hang my head. *What am I supposed to say, that I'd still been under the spell of my evil birth mother?* "I wanted a ringside seat to the police arresting them. I didn't mean to actually go inside."

Raul rolls his eyes at me, then rubs his chin. "I know how we could try to get it from them, safely, if your navigation skills are still in working order."

"Huh?"

"The map, Andreo."

I fish the map out of my pack. My parents hadn't needed it to bike to Cochabamba—or so I'd reasoned to myself when I'd taken off with our team's only copy.

Raul points to two penciled Xs I don't remember marking. "When Maria and I fooled around on our day off . . ."

I laugh. He blushes, a rare sight on Raul.

"I mean, when she took me to a couple of caves around Torotoro . . ."

"Yeah?"

"There was one that joined up with the big cave that they're in now—Caverna Refugio. This X marks the big cave, and this one the tunnel. The cave and tunnel join up just like that tunnel did with the big cave back home in Canmore."

"You mean a tunnel up to a grizzly bear's behind?"

"If that's what you want to call our party of three desperadoes."

My heartbeat picks up as I consider that. "You're saying there's a secret-passage tunnel up to their lair? We crawl up it, wait till they're asleep and nab the notebook?"

"Something like that. The tunnel joins the big cave through a hole about the size of an air vent. Nothing grown men would notice or try and crawl through, but doable for us."

"Not even Vanessa would fit?"

Raul sneers. "She might break a fingernail or scuff her heels."

I smile. Just like something my mother would say. If I had to choose between Mother and Vanessa in a tight situation, my adoptive mother would win, hands down. "So, if two salamanders hang out at the vent, they can see and hear everything without being spotted."

"Best seat in the theater."

"But the police. Shouldn't we ride down and inform them?" I ask.

"You already left a message with Colque; he's sure to have phoned them by now."

"But how will he and the police know where Vanessa and Vargas are if they're not in the shack anymore?"

"I'm way ahead of you on that," says Raul smugly. "I've already left a note on the Jeep's windshield."

I shake my head, whip out my compass and hold the map's smaller *X* close to my face. "Andreo's Navigation is at your service."

CHAPTER NINETEEN

It takes twenty minutes for me to track down the tunnel entrance. We stash our bikes, shoulder our packs and enter. I reflect how nice it is to be out of the rain as we advance through a relatively spacious series of passages. Soon, however, things get tighter, and the ceiling becomes so low that we're forced to tie our packs to our feet and drag them behind us. As we crawl on our hands and knees, our headlamps illuminate interesting patterns of sculpted rock.

"This is cool," I whisper.

"Yeah," Raul replies. "Maria knows so many cool caves around here. She's amazing."

I grin. "So I hear."

Where the passageway gets even tighter, we drop to our stomachs and elbows and proceed in single file ever upward until we hear voices ahead. Bingo! So this really is the back entrance to Caverna Refugio. We switch off our headlamps and breathe as quietly as we can, wriggling forward much more slowly and cautiously. Finally, we stop at a slight widening, untie our packs from our feet and lie squashed side by side a safe distance back from the opening, which is marked by the faint light of a lantern across the cavern.

I smell dirt, sulfur, body odor and beer. *Beer?* As my eyes adjust to the dark, I see that directly in front of us, his body half-blocking the vent-size exit, is the reclining figure of the tattooed guard. His deep breathing indicates he's asleep. To his left are two empty plastic bottles of *chicha*. In his lap lies a handgun.

Though I can't see Raul's face in the dark, I can almost hear our heartbeats pick up. It's not too late to slide backward, retreat, abandon this mission. Angling my head a little more, I see Vargas and Vanessa sitting on their suitcase, the lantern beside them. Vargas is holding the record book.

"Burn it," Vanessa is pleading.

Vargas heaves a big sigh. "I guess we should." He hesitates. "Our life's work." He looks at his watch. "Where is he? He said he was on his way half an hour ago."

"He'll come," Vanessa says. She leans her head against Vargas's shoulders and closes her eyes. He wraps an arm around her and presses his lips to her cheek.

I feel Raul fidgeting beside me. He's fishing something out of his pack, then inching forward. My mouth falls open as, in the shadowy light, I see him reach out to replace the guard's two empty containers of beer with the two full ones he took from the shack. He has even opened them for the guard. Seconds later, Raul is back beside me and stuffing Jorge's empties into his pack. My eyes fly to Vargas and Vanessa, but there's no sign they've noticed.

A particularly loud snore from Jorge makes Vargas shout at the guard. "Jorge, wake up. We're not paying you to nap."

Jorge stirs, slurs a curse or two and sits up straighter. We watch his hand reach for a bottle. We hear him chug the entire beer down, belch and start in on the second. Though I can't see Raul's face, I can pretty much bet he's grinning. While visiting his house, I had often seen him hide beer from his parents. Tonight, he's in reverse mode. We slide backward a few feet for safety's sake and wait. We lie there for what may be minutes or hours. I may even have dozed off myself when I feel Raul's elbow in my side. He leans very close to whisper into my ear, "Get the gun."

Huh? I come fully awake. I blanch as I realize what Raul is asking. Looking toward our vent, I see that Jorge has moved his gun from his lap to the cavern floor beside him. He's snoring softly. I reach backward to my pack and feel my trekking pole. Then I unfold it, slide forward as soundlessly as I can and peer across the spacious room. Vargas is slumped against the cavern wall, eyes closed. Vanessa is curled up on their suitcase, head resting on her knitting bag, asleep as well.

I push my pole forward, inch by inch, trying to keep

it steady despite my shaking arm. It reaches the gun, floats over it, eases down to capture it. Slowly, ever so slowly, I slide it back. The second the gun arrives within reach, Raul grabs it and squirms backward at high speed, leaving me within pole's reach of a drunken guard we've just robbed.

Some muffled clicking behind me makes me wonder, terrified, what my crazy friend is doing. When I hear the ping of metal hitting rock, I stare out our hole, thinking we're done for now. But the slumber party remains intact. Then I feel the cold metal of the gun pressed into my hand, which scares me so much I nearly drop it.

"Ease it back," Raul is whispering as he stuffs bullets from the gun's magazine into his backpack. My teeth are locked together; my nerves are running an electrical current from my jaw to my toes. But I crawl forward as far as I dare, place the gun on the tunnel floor and push it gently forward with my pole. A loud hiccup from Jorge almost gives me a heart attack. I hold my breath as the guard stirs, letting it out again only when he settles back to dreaming. I continue the pole push until the gun is back where it was, then retract my pole and sink into a sweaty mess.

Sometime later I wake to the smell of cigar smoke drifting into Raul's and my cramped hideaway. Raising my head, I see Vargas not just smoking but also flicking his lighter off and on while cradling the yellow notebook in his lap.

"Do it," Vanessa orders. "Burn it now."

I'm about to elbow Raul in the ribs when I feel him rise beside me and launch himself out of the vent, right over a startled Jorge. Raul, with the element of surprise on his side, manages to close his fingers over the notebook and wrest it from Vargas's grasp just as it catches fire.

Then everything happens at once. Vanessa shouts, Vargas lunges after Raul and I push my fists and helmeted head full strength into Jorge's backside as he tries to stumble to his feet. Jorge falls heavily, knocking his head on the cave floor. I step out from the tunnel and observe, with a stab of guilt, that he's out cold. Meanwhile, Vargas's heavyset body, no match for Raul's fleet feet, fails to prevent Raul from sprinting to the vent, then dropping the notebook to stamp out the flames and flinging it down our tunnel's length like he's competing in a Frisbee championship.

Smart thinking, I realize. No one but us will be able to retrieve it from there!

As for me, the minute Vargas's beady eyes lock on me, I let unknown instincts take over: I pick up the fallen guard's handgun, point it at the fat man and cock it. Vargas and Vanessa stop in their tracks, mouths dropping open.

"Raul," I order, "peel some duct tape off my trekking pole and tape Jorge's hands behind his back before he comes to." I don't know whether the guard is drunk, concussed or both, but even if the gun were loaded—and I remind myself that Vargas and Vanessa don't know it's not—I consider two irate adults enough to deal with.

"Jorge!" Vargas shouts as Raul kneels and begins a lightning-fast duct-tape job on the man's wrists and ankles. "Get up, you drunk, before it's too late!" Then he turns to me and switches to the soothing, patient voice I've come to hate. "Andreo, have you any idea how dangerous a firearm can be?"

I do my best imitation of his belly laugh. "You think kids who live in grizzly bear and moose country don't get taught pretty young how to handle a simple piece like this?" That shuts him up.

"Andreo," Vanessa pleads, taking a step toward me. "Don't get yourself hurt. Put the gun down, son."

"I am not your son," I bark, aiming the empty gun point-blank at her; she does a hasty retreat. "You mean nothing to me, Mrs. Vargas. My real parents taught me right from wrong. That's why I know it's up to me to shut you down. You chose your fate when you joined Vargas's business. Now all I want is to see both of you arrested."

Raul, kneeling on the moaning Jorge like the guard is his personal bear trophy, raises his eyebrows at my speech and smiles.

I see Vargas edging toward the lantern beside the red suitcase. He thinks it might be clever to plunge us all into darkness? I reach up to flick my helmet headlamp on and shine it right into his face. Raul does the same. Vargas blinks and freezes.

"Boys!" comes a booming voice at the cave entrance. We turn to see someone carrying a second lantern. A hint of cologne enters my nostrils. *Detective Colque!* I'm so relieved I could sink to the floor on the spot.

CHAPTER TWENTY

"*Increíble!*" Colque enthuses, shaking his head as he surveys the scene. "You boys are hired anytime you want to move to Cochabamba. Not that you *should* have been taking matters into your own hands, mind you. How'd you pull this off?"

"Snuck up that tunnel," I say proudly, pointing.

"Where they dared to throw my record book a moment ago," Vargas grouses.

"Where are the police?" Raul asks Colque.

"Right behind me," the detective says. I feel my body relax even more.

Colque walks over and uses the toe of his boot to lift Jorge's chin. "Drunk? Vargas, can't you even hire a decent guard? And, Vanessa, how did I miss your secret connection to Vargas all these years?"

She stares blandly at him. Vargas crosses his arms and glares at the detective.

"Raul, you sure are handy with a roll of duct tape," the

detective continues. "Nice work. Andreo, hand the gun to me and I'll take over from here."

I give him the gun, even though I'm momentarily stunned by Raul shouting, "No! Don't, Andreo!"

The detective, gun in hand, keeps it leveled at Vanessa and Vargas as if he didn't hear Raul's outburst. "Okay, Andreo, all we need now is the notebook. Can you fetch that for me?"

"As soon as the police arrive," Raul answers for me in a steely voice. I look at him in surprise. *What kind of answer is that?*

The detective has turned to survey Raul closely, his eyes narrowed. Raul's forehead reveals beads of sweat, and I know my friend's full-on stare at me is trying to communicate something. But all I am is confused.

Detective's Colque's tone turns sharp. "No time to play games, Raul. Andreo, be a good *muchacho* and—"

"You're not working for the Cochabamba police, are you?" Raul demands.

"Of course I am, Raul," the detective responds, looking puzzled and hurt. "And we established right from the start that my mission is to bring Vargas to justice."

"Isn't it handy that your office in Cochabamba is right beside Vargas's vacated one?" Raul asks, his voice dripping sarcasm. I begin to feel alarmed. *What's Raul suddenly on to that I've missed?*

"I hoped it would help me connect with people like you and Andreo, as I told you when we first met," Colque says patiently, "so we could find adoptive parents willing to testify and help connect adoptees and birth parents where possible."

"You mean identify anyone who *might* be willing to testify, so you could intimidate them out of the idea like you did with Ardillita and Juan Pedro," Raul accuses, eyes flashing at the detective. "And *pretend* to put adoptees in touch with birth parents while really doing everything you can to prevent them from finding each other."

"Raul, you're not making sense!" I object.

Raul ignores me. "You put Andreo and Vanessa together eventually, but only after we phoned and told you that we'd met Ardillita and Juan Pedro and that Ardillita had spotted Vanessa in the village. And only after you'd phoned Vargas to tell him all that, correct? Am I also right that Vargas okayed your setting up a meeting, and then the two of you coached his wife on what to say, in hopes of satisfying Andreo? 'You'll return to Canada satisfied' is what you said to Andreo. You figured that meeting would throw us off the scent long enough to help your real bosses, Hugo and Vanessa Vargas, get out of the country. How much is Vargas paying you, anyway?"

I'm looking from Colque to Vargas to Vanessa. No one is responding, but Colque's gun—had I really been so stupid that I handed it to him?—slowly swings from the couple to Raul. *Thank goodness Raul emptied it* is all I can think.

"Hurry this up and let's get out of here," Vargas orders Colque in Spanish as he strides across the cave like someone intent on grabbing hold of us. "What took you so long, anyway?"

It occurs to me—and I'm guessing to Raul too—that we should dash to the tunnel entrance and dive down it, right now. But Colque, reading my mind, steps between us and the tunnel until Vargas's large hands close around Raul's arms. "Good," says Colque. "Hold Raul while Andreo squeezes into that tunnel to retrieve the notebook, Hugo."

Raul and I exchange looks. I do a quick shake of my head to stop him from calling a bluff on the gun yet.

"No, let Raul get the notebook," I say firmly. "He's the better caver. And after you hand it over, Raul, show Detective Colque what we've discovered hydration pack tubes can be used for."

Raul's response is a bare hint of a smile. I don't expect him to get down the tunnel and up to the detective's truck fast enough to siphon his gas, but if the police aren't on their way and things are about to take a turn for the worse in this cavern, it's better that at least one of us and that notebook stay safe.

The detective looks momentarily confused. "If that's code for doing something funny, I'd strongly advise against it," he says. "Especially since I've got Andreo here as hostage."

Vargas has yet to release Raul. I do a fast calculation. Even with the gun disabled and Jorge out of action, I know better than to try and dodge three adults in an escape attempt, especially before Raul is free of Vargas.

"Clever boy, aren't you?" Colque says to Raul. "But why should you care who I'm working for? I helped Andreo meet his birth mother, and now you're headed back home. All's well that ends well."

"Not," I say, prompting Vargas's evil eye to shift to me. Vanessa, meanwhile, moves back to the suitcase and plunks down tiredly.

"We're not actually headed home till this ring is history," I say, causing Vargas to laugh. "And maybe I have a few questions too. Like who came up with the beauty queen and married doctor line?" *Buying time. Hurry up, Police Chief Ferreira.*

"Me!" says Vargas proudly. "It was half true for my first client—you—and seemed to please your adoptive parents."

"It worked so well that I advised him to use it on all our adoptive parent clients," Colque adds, grinning.

"Not very original by the six hundredth baby," I say dryly. "So I know why Dr. A was so willing to loan his clinic for the meeting. All four of you were in on this. How many people are working for you, anyway, Mr. Vargas?"

No response from the boss.

"It also explains why no one was at the shack when you first drove us up there," Raul addresses Colque bitterly. "You'd tipped them off in time for them to leave. And it's no wonder you never phoned the police like you said you were going to—then or now." *So why is Ferreira in Torotoro?* I wonder. *For Raul and me?* If so, they won't know to check out the shack, let alone this cave.

Colque and Vargas smile. Vanessa, frowning, has returned to her knitting as if to avoid everyone's eyes. With each furious stitch, the thick blue hat is coming off her needles, like she's done with it.

Memories are racing through my mind: Colque breezily informing us there was no charge for his services, and that we didn't need our adoptive parents' permission for him to help us. His e-mailing me that Vanessa was born in a small village near Cochabamba, but not replying to my question, *What small village?* His not knowing—or pretending not to know—that Vanessa and Vargas were married. And his assurance that *Vargas would never hurt Vanessa.*

"So all those times you asked whether my adoptive parents might be willing to testify," I say, my blood pumping as fast as Vanessa's needles, "you were just double-checking that they weren't. And all those questions about our race route were to keep track of us. You must have been pretty nervous when you learned it went through Torotoro."

"It wouldn't have been a problem if you hadn't hooked up with Ardillita somehow," Colque replies evenly. "Release Raul, Hugo, and let him fetch the notebook if he doesn't want his friend to get hurt."

"I won't let them hurt you, Andreo," Raul says soberly before crawling into our vent.

———

Things go quiet after Raul disappears down the tunnel—deadly quiet as we wait. Vargas, Vanessa and the detective are all sweating like they're in a sauna, if my powers of observation are worth anything. Long after my friend should have returned, Vargas orders Vanessa to move to the hole and shine their lantern down it. She does as he asks.

"Gone," she says resignedly. "I told you we should have burned the notebook earlier." She returns to the suitcase as if awaiting the next order.

"He has run off. Is that what you think too, Andreo?" Colque asks me, voice rising. "Maybe he doesn't consider you such a good friend after all."

I hang my head like I'm devastated and back away like I'm frightened.

"Hugo," Colque directs calmly, his stare at me icy, "get your suitcase and your wife in my truck and get the hell gone. I'll cut Jorge free, take care of Andreo and get back to town somehow."

"Don't you hurt him," Vanessa's voice floats across the cave.

"Shall I shoot him?" Colque asks Vargas, ignoring her.

"Whatever you think is best," Vargas replies indifferently as he picks up the suitcase and lantern. "The other boy has nothing but a half-burned notebook. We'll be safe before anyone can do anything with it."

Vanessa walks over to me, her skirt swishing, her low-heeled silver sandals making hollow clicks on the stone floor. She lifts the thick blue hat from her knitting bag and offers it with outstretched hands and something like warmth in her eyes.

I accept it with trembling hands. "Thanks," I whisper. "I'm glad we met, even if—"

She places one of her manicured fingernails on my lips to stop me from finishing. Then she goes on tiptoes to kiss the top of my head. "Lead a good life, my son, and love your adoptive parents."

In my suddenly blurred vision, she steps in front of me and faces Colque, deliberately blocking the aim of Colque's gun.

"Put the gun down, Diego," she commands.

"Vanessa!" Vargas objects.

"Hugo, I'm not moving until he does."

"But Vanessa, sweetest . . ."

"Put it down," she repeats, louder.

Colque looks from Vargas to her, finally receiving a reluctant signal from Vargas to do as Vanessa says. Slowly, he places it at his feet. Vanessa moves quickly to pick it up, stuffs it into her knitting bag and marches over to her annoyed husband. Then, without a backward glance at me, she trails Vargas and their muddied suitcase out into the rain.

"Thanks, Mom," I mumble, and recall something Ardillita said: *Remember, no mother can forget or stop loving, even if she's forced to hide the pain deep in her heart.*

Without taking his eyes off me, Colque produces a knife from his pocket and leans down to cut Jorge free.

While I fondle the new hat, I mentally measure the distances between me and the main cave entrance and me and the tunnel.

Colque, after inspecting Jorge's head, slaps him hard across his cheek.

"Don't!" comes a drunken wail.

"Wake up, you useless *borracho*," Colque says—Spanish for "drunk." "I need your help to corner this devil." He turns toward me and wields his knife. Jorge rises, the patch of dried blood on his forehead a perfect match with his angry, bloodshot eyes.

I lean down to pick up a loose rock and, taking careful note of where the two men stand, fling it full force at Colque's lantern. As it shatters, I shut off my own headlamp.

Though all three of us are now blind as bats, I'm betting only one of us has something close to a bat's finely tuned senses and echolocation navigational skills. The sound of the rain identifies the cave's entrance. Subtle air currents point me toward the vent. Jorge's stumbling and the reek of beer proclaim his movements. And Colque, however stealthy he thinks he's being, is betrayed by his cologne.

For five tense minutes, we circle each other in the humid blackness like wrestlers at the start of a match. At one point, Jorge lunges and lashes out with extended fists, catching me in the right eye as I spin away. It stings like hell, will be a real shiner, but I dodge Colque's follow-up attempt to corner me. Instead, I make my break for it, sprinting for the vent and diving down it. Like an adventure-race pro, I flick my headlamp on, grab my backpack and wriggle down the length of the shaft to leap on my bike. Then I head up in the hammering rain toward the road that ends at the shack.

Giving my instincts full rein, I pedal through dripping, scratchy brush as fast as I can. I'm aiming for the darkened shack, after which I'll look for Colque's vehicle—and hopefully find Raul—while remaining on alert for Vargas and Vanessa's lantern. I'm so intent on my mission that I fail to identify a solid object before slamming into it: a tall, strong body that wraps its arms around me and flops me forcefully to the ground.

"Good evening, Andreo. You seem to be in an awful hurry. You may remember that we've met. I'm Police Chief Ferreira."

CHAPTER TWENTY-ONE

"Police Chief Ferreira, I'm so glad to . . . ," I begin.

"We have Raul."

"You have Raul? What do you mean?"

"You'll see."

He takes me firmly by one shoulder, allowing me to haul my bike beside me with my other hand, and hustles me up the hill, lecturing me along the way: ". . . got in over your head . . . frightened your parents half to death . . . caused a scandal for the adventure-race organizer."

As we near the hut, the lights of two police squad cars and a police van pierce the falling rain. Ferreira maneuvers me toward one of the cars. Inside, I see a cop in the driver's seat and three figures in the screened-off backseat. A rear window rolls down as we approach. Raul, his dreadlocks a wet mess, sticks his head out.

"Hey, Andreo. Glad you could join the party." His cheerfulness sounds a bit forced. I move closer and my jaw loosens when I see that he's squished back there beside

Vanessa and Vargas, whose eyes refuse to meet mine. Silently, the couple are studying the handcuffs that lock them together.

Ferreira's grip on me remains firm.

Raul's driver opens his door, steps out and nods at Ferreira.

"Andreo, meet Tirotoro Sheriff Benito Savedra," Ferreira says. "Benito, this is Andreo."

The sheriff sticks his hand out; I grip it weakly. "*Um, hola,*" I say. "What's going on?"

That's when Raul decides to fill me in. "So, first the sheriff here jumps out of nowhere and arrests me for trying to siphon gas. Then he locks me in the back of this cruiser for being the handsome mug on one of his WANTED posters."

I flash a look at Savedra; he doesn't look amused.

"And as if that's not bad enough, ten minutes later he stuffs Vanessa and Vargas in the back of the car with me. Luckily they're handcuffed or they'd be seriously pummeling me to get the notebook I've still got."

Raul's grin lights up his rain-soaked face. Vargas scowls, but Vanessa keeps her eyes on her lap.

"That's enough, Raul," Ferreira says. "You two can talk back at the station. In fact, you'll be doing plenty of talking. Andreo, load your bike in the police van beside Raul's bike, please."

Sheriff Savedra pushes the button on his door that rolls up Raul's window, then positions himself back in the driver's seat and closes the door. After I've stowed my bike, Ferreira guides me to the second squad car, opens the rear door and directs me in. There's an officer at the wheel who eyes me sullenly in his rearview mirror.

"Buckle up," Ferreira instructs, then slams my door closed and disappears into the wet night. I try the handle—locked. My driver makes no move to drive off; I can hear Raul's car also idling.

"Why aren't we going?" I ask my driver in Spanish.

"More people joining us," he says.

We don't have long to wait. In the car's headlights, I soon see Ferreira and two more officers stride past my car, Colque and Jorge in cuffs between them and David at Ferreira's side.

David? What's he doing here?

Through the rain-streaked windshield, I watch Ferreira and the officers load Colque and Jorge into the back of the police van and the officers climb in after them.

The two far doors of my car creak open.

"Hey, bro," David says casually as he plops into the seat beside me.

"Let's go," Ferreira directs the driver of our car as he takes the front passenger seat.

"What are you doing here?" I ask my brother, unable to disguise my shock.

"Helping the police find you," he answers evenly. "You want the whole story?"

"*Um*, yeah," I say as our car bounces down the road.

"Well, back at the caves, after you and Raul jumped into that shuttle truck without us, Mom, Dad and I cut in line to get on the very next ride. At the bike vans, when we found your note, Mom and Dad wanted to chase you down, but I said if your birth mother lived in Torotoro, you'd lied and were headed back there, not to Cochabamba."

"You guessed right," I say, lowering my head.

"Obviously. Anyway, Dad told one of the bike-van drivers that this was an emergency. He asked him to drive ahead, check if you guys were on the road, then phone us on our satellite phone."

"Dad broke open our satellite phone?" I ask.

"Yup, thereby disqualifying our team. When the guy phoned and said there was no sign of you, Mom, Dad and I biked to Torotoro at breakneck speed. We met Maria coming from the other direction. She had no idea what you were up to, but lent us her map when she found out we didn't have one."

"Sorry, I figured you didn't need it to bike back to Cochabamba," I say sheepishly.

"At the Torotoro police station, Mom downloaded photos of you two—"

"And they put up posters," I fill in.

"I'd just arrived at the Torotoro police station," Ferreira speaks up, "because of an earlier tip about Vargas. Sheriff Savedra and I were about to head out to check on suspected hideouts when David insisted on coming along."

"I'd noticed two *X*s on Maria's map by then," David says. "I thought maybe they might be a clue to where you were."

"The cave and tunnel, I'm guessing," I say. "Raul made the same *X*s on our map the morning he and Maria went caving."

"So David rode up here with us," Ferreira says, "and his map-reading skills led us toward the cave, which is how we found Jorge's Jeep and Colque's 4x4 down the road from the shack. Also Raul's note confirming that that was where you were. Then David did some pretty impressive navigating in the dark and rain to lead us to this Caverna Refugio place, which even Sheriff Savedra had never heard of."

"Way to go, David," I say with genuine pride.

My brother's smile is just visible.

"He kept making us stand ahead, one at a time, to take compass bearings off us and count out paces for some kind of mathematical formula," Ferreira said.

"Learned from the best," David mumbles as our car pulls up to the Torotoro police station.

"And now," Ferreira says, "it's time for some debriefing, Andreo, before you and Raul rejoin your family."

CHAPTER TWENTY-TWO

Two hours later, we're sitting on some overstuffed red sofas in the Torotoro hotel lobby: Dad, Mother, David, Raul, me, Police Chief Ferreira and Sheriff Savedra. Raul and I have recounted our stories to the officers at the Torotoro police station—who'd actually been pretty decent while grilling us—and now we're filling in my family.

"So, this Detective Colque," Dad addresses me. "How was it that Raul figured out he was part of Vargas's operation and you didn't?"

Raul answers before I can: "When Andreo dozed off in the tunnel, I overheard Vargas say to Vanessa, 'Colque should be here by now.' I was shocked for a minute, but then I started to think about all the things that hadn't been adding up about Colque, especially his not calling the police the time he drove us to the shack. Vargas started burning the notebook before I got a chance to tell Andreo. I tried to stop Andreo from handing Colque the gun, but Andreo can be a bit slow at times," he says, making a face at me.

"And *not* slow at times," David pipes up. "He was faster and smarter than Colque and that Jorge guy at the end, or he might have gotten knifed. And his navigational skills got you to the secret tunnel entrance in the first place."

My brother is actually sticking up for me? Even sounding proud of me? I swallow and look from my parents to David. "Mother, Dad, David, I am really, really sorry for putting you through all this. All we ever meant to do was a bit of research on our birth parents, if we could. I shouldn't have stolen documents out of the safe—"

"We should never have kept them from you, Andreo," Dad says, hanging his head. "Nor the hat. I told your mother that, years ago."

"It was my fault," she says, moving a hand slowly, hesitantly toward mine. I grasp it and lean in to kiss her cheek. She looks so startled, she doesn't speak for a moment; then she lifts her other hand to her face to wipe away a tear. "When we first adopted you," she says in almost a whisper, "I had a feeling something wasn't right about it. The cost, the way Mr. Vargas did things, his overly smooth manner. But we'd wanted a baby for so long, and there were too few babies to adopt, too much demand in North America. We were convinced this was the only way. . . ."

"I'm afraid I bought into Vargas's business—hook, line and sinker," my father says, frowning. "I never suspected it was an illegal operation; I thought your mother was being overly paranoid."

"When you cried so much, I thought maybe you knew . . . ," Mother says.

"Knew?" I echo when she pauses.

"Knew you'd been stolen, if you were. Knew I wasn't your real mother. Hated me for what we'd done."

"Hated you?" I turn to face the mother who has raised me, the mother I now realize has loved me fiercely all my life. "Seriously, Mother, Dad, David, I've learned this week who my real family is. It was stupid to go chasing after some fairy-tale mom. Who turned out to be worse than an evil stepmother." I grin weakly.

"Told you so," Raul inserts helpfully.

"Not so evil," Mother says, stroking my hair. "First of all, she gifted us with you sixteen years ago. Second, she tried to save your life in the cave. Third, she made you a nice hat. She's quite a talented knitter. Maybe I will have to take up a new hobby."

She fingers my new blue hat thoughtfully. "I'm sorry for heaping so much guilt and blame on myself that I've never been much of a mother to you, Andreo."

"That is not true, Mother—*er*, Mom. Can I call you Mom instead of Mother? Mother is so formal."

She laughs and says, "Of course, Andreo."

I turn and wrap my arm around her with a force that surprises both of us. I lean my wet face into her wet face and whisper, "I love you. And I'm so, so sorry for all this."

"Hey," Dad pipes up. "What about me?"

I wrap my other arm around him, and we have a bear hug. A grizzly bear hug. David says, "Family love-in, huh? Well, guess I'd better jump in." And he does.

The skinny girl serving as the hotel receptionist gawks, but I don't care.

"Okay, this is getting way too soppy for me," Raul states.

"About that note you left on the bikes," Dad says as we release one another.

I feel my face flush red. "I flat-out lied," I admit. "I'm really sorry. I lied in order to buy Raul and me more time in Torotoro while you finished the race. I knew how important it was for you to finish. I figured unranked was better than nothing."

"You thought finishing the race was more important than being a family?" Dad shakes his head in disbelief. "You thought finishing was so big a deal we'd still do it after you had run away?"

"I—I guess I did."

Dad looks devastated. "Andreo, Andreo, my son. I know I was angry earlier, but only because I hadn't had time to think it through. I should have realized how wrong it was to act like you weren't adopted and hide your birth information from you. I thought I was protecting your mother's feelings. But surely you know that neither David nor I meant what we said about time-outs and going unranked."

"That was my fault," David cuts in. "I knew you guys had been sneaking around, and I felt left out. I shouldn't have snooped in your backpack, but the whole birth certificate thing really threw me when I did. I was shocked and crazy-angry at what you and Raul had been doing. And super scared that Mom was going to be hurt when she found out. So what did I do? Something even stupider—I got into a shouting match with you that *made* her find out. And I said things I really, really didn't mean, like telling you we could go unranked and that you didn't fit into our family."

He walks over to me and places his hands on my shoulders. "You have no idea how freaked out I was when I realized you really had taken off. Andreo, I know I can be a total pain of a brother, and I'll try to be nicer if you will. But, well, I don't really want to be an only child." He cracks a half-smile.

I nod and punch his shoulder lightly. He drops his arms back to his sides.

"Don't you dare run away again," he says in a tight voice, "'cause you know I'm not as fast—I won't be able to catch you."

"That's true," I kid him.

CHAPTER TWENTY-THREE

"So, after David left with Police Chief Ferreira and Sheriff Savedra," Dad continues, "the rest of us came to the hotel here, booked two rooms and waited for word."

"You can't imagine how relieved we were when Chief Ferreira phoned to say he'd found you two," Mom says. "Then we had to wait here forever until the police were done questioning you."

Everyone goes quiet for a few minutes, totally spent.

"Well, it has been one hell of an adventure race for your team," Ferreira finally says. "And a very successful day for me. May I be so bold as to ask whether you, Mr. and Mrs. Wilson, might be willing to make a statement on adopting through Hugo Vargas?"

"Yes," Mom and Dad say together. I feel a surge of pride.

Ferreira turns to Raul. "And you, Raul, did you find anything in that notebook I confiscated from you about your birth parents? Unfortunately, Colque and the Vargases categorically refuse to answer that question."

Mom, Dad, David and I turn to study Raul's face, which has fallen.

"*Nah.* I knew it wasn't in the cards. Like I said, they're probably worse than my—"

"What is your birth mother's name, son?" Savedra asks.

"Adriana Apaza."

The shcriff's eyes widen. His mouth opens slightly. "And your birth date?"

Raul mumbles his answer.

Savedra turns to Ferreira. "Excuse me for a moment." He rises and lopes out the hotel's front door, watched by the bored receptionist.

"So, David," I say, "I guess while we're doing apologies, I'm sorry I spent my life being jealous of you for being the favorite, natural-born son."

"Jealous? Favorite?" David scratches his head. "I've spent my whole life being jealous of your being so good at sports—which I imagined made you Mom and Dad's favorite."

"We don't have favorites!" Dad declares, extending his long, strong arms to the backs of both our necks and pretending to slam our heads together.

"That's true, David and Andreo," Mom says, her tone serious. "And we've got the rest of our lives to do better at demonstrating it."

"Well, you could say we're your twins again, Mom," I joke, pointing to David's and my black-and-blue eyes.

"*Hmmm,*" she says. "Not my idea of—"

"Good family dynamics," Dad fills in, winking at Raul.

"Right," Raul says, looking at David. "I apologize for punching you in the face."

"Apology accepted. And I promise not to hit on any of your girlfriends again. Though you have better taste than I imagined."

The lobby door flies open, and Ardillita and Juan Pedro bustle into the room, their five-year-old boy in Juan Pedro's arms. They're trailed by Savedra. The couple look from one to the other of us, then move to stand in front of Raul.

"You must be Raul." Ardillita drops to her knees and takes Raul's hand in hers.

He looks at her like she's nuts.

"They told me you were a girl just out of spite," she says in a shaky voice. "They told me that to make my search more difficult. And I believed them."

Raul's face has frozen in shock. "But the birth certificate says—"

"Adriana Apaza. Ardillita is short for Adriana; it's a nickname. Apaza was my maiden name. And Juan Pedro . . ."

She breaks off as Juan Pedro sets the little boy down, grabs both of Raul's hands and pulls him to his feet. "Son, we're so happy to finally find you." His voice is deep and emotional. He pulls Raul into a man-to-man hug. From the corner of my eyes, I see the hotel lobby receptionist grimace like she's about to make a phone call to admit us all to an insane asylum. When Raul falls back into his seat, the five-year-old climbs into his lap, looks at him with big eyes and runs a finger through his dreadlocks.

Ardillita laughs. "Moises, this is Raul, your brother. Raul, meet Moises."

"Brother," Raul repeats, testing out the word.

"Mrs. de los Angeles is looking after the rest. This one wouldn't go to sleep so we brought him with us."

Raul's face transforms from shock to glowing. He lifts a finger and brushes the boy's hair away from his eyes, then hums Bob Marley to him. Soon, the boy falls asleep, allowing Raul and his birth parents to talk in low tones. *If anyone deserves a fairy-tale ending, it is Raul,* I think to myself, only a little choked up.

Ferreira coughs. "*Um,* not to break this up, but it's getting close to midnight and I have to head back to Cochabamba early in the morning. I need to be there in time to greet the first finishers."

"The first finishers," Dad muses.

"Hey, we could hitch a ride with you and get there in time to *be* the first finishers!" David jokes.

Ferreira laughs. "Not sure about that, but you could get there in time to see your friend Maria McLeod come in. I can even make room for the bikes."

Raul's head comes up at the sound of Maria's name. Juan Pedro grins like he knows why. "I have an idea," he says to his birth son. "How about we collect Mrs. de los

Angeles and our kids at first light and head up in my truck for a day in Cochabamba? Mrs. de los Angeles can see her sons and granddaughter come in, and you can ride with us."

"Yes, please!" Raul says. "Maybe we can join in the post-race party."

"I'm all for that!" Dad says. "We earned the party, even if we didn't finish, did we not?"

"I'll vouch for you," Ferreira says.

"We finished high in the family category," Mom declares, squeezing my hand.

Everyone stands. I stretch, yawn and amble over to Raul. "Looks like we're going our separate ways," I say. "I mean to Cochabamba tomorrow morning."

"Yeah," he says, doing a lousy job of hiding a goofy smile. "But it's been real, *mon*. See you at the finish line."

"Have a good ride up, Raul Espada. You've been a first-class partner in adventure and crime. *Misión completa*."

"Mission complete," he agrees.

ACKNOWLEDGMENTS

Above all, I am indebted to my researcher, Richie (Jonathan Borda Gutierrez) of Cochabamba, Bolivia, a runner/bicyclist/hiker/Bob Marley fan and adoptee who has unbridled enthusiasm for life and adventure. Through months of e-mails, he patiently answered my questions, helped choose the racecourse and sports and named many of the characters. He also supplied me with a six-page, extensively detailed (from geology and climate to people's dress) *diario* and almost a hundred photos of his ten-hour, super-bumpy round-trip bus ride to Torotoro National Park and his stay there. In the region, he spent several days caving in some of the dozens of caverns (there really is a matrimonial cave) and exploring surrounding villages and terrain (including the fiberglass dinosaur in Torotoro's village square). Later, when I arrived in Cochabamba, he accompanied me to Villa Tunari and Sucre, serving as guide, Spanish tutor, translator and all-round, fun-loving friend.

That being said, I'd like to make it clear that parts of the racecourse in this novel are fictional and that no one—repeat no one—should even think about bicycling the highway between Cochabamba and Villa Tunari. (Driving it is hair-raising enough!)

Sincere thanks also go to adventure race organizer Bryan Tasaka (Mind Over Mountain, Vancouver, Canada), who made himself available to answer many questions about the sport. Also to Martin Sellens, expert orienteer; Malcolm Scruggs, my valued teen editor; Silvana Bevilacqua, my sharp-eyed friend; Steve, my husband and fellow adventurer; and Ren Gregoire and her family, Jord and Ayrton.

Last but certainly not least, sincere thanks to my literary agent, Lynn Bennett; to editor Sue Tate and all the team at Tundra Books; to my speaking tours agent, Chris Patrick (www.pamwithers.com); and to my readers.

ABOUT THE AUTHOR

Pam Withers is the critically acclaimed author of sixteen best-selling adventure novels for teens, including the award-winning *First Descent*. An outdoor enthusiast and mother, Pam is a former whitewater raft guide, kayak racer, kids' summer camp coordinator, journalist, editor and associate publisher. She is also co-founder of www.keenreaders.org and co-author of *Jump-Starting Boys: Help Your Reluctant Learner Find Success in School and Life*. Pam lives in Vancouver, British Columbia, with her husband, when not touring to speak on her books or on boys and literacy. Visit her website at www.pamwithers.com.

PRAISE FOR *FIRST DESCENT* BY PAM WITHERS

"Withers, who has built her reputation as a writer of YA sports adventures, gets things moving quickly . . . and when the action starts to flow, the ride is fast and furious."
— *Quill & Quire*

"From the first page . . . Withers flings the reader from one perilous adventure to another."
— *Booklist*

"Reluctant readers will especially enjoy the adventure."
— *School Library Journal*